The Journey of Hector Rabinal

Dudley Watt

THE JOURNEY OF
HECTOR RABINAL

A NOVEL BY

DONLEY WATT

Texas Christian University Press
Fort Worth

Library of Congress Cataloging-in-Publication Data

Watt, Donley.
  The journey of Hector Rabinal : a novel / by Donley Watt.
        p. cm.
  ISBN 0- 87565- 125- 9
  1. Peasantry — Guatemala — Fiction. 2. Guatemalans — Texas
— Fiction.
I. Title.
PS3573.A8585J68   1994
813'.54 — dc20

                                                        93- 30375
                                                             CIP

Cover art and book design by Barbara Whitehead

For Lynn

PROLOGUE

MY NAME IS Bartolo Mendez Cota. I am a Guatemalan by birth and except for the past three of my sixty-seven years have never lived out of my country. As a young man I trained for the priesthood, for reasons that were apparent at the time but seem not so apparent now. After several years I left the church. Again the reasons at the time seemed clear but now are diluted. I returned to my village of Huitupan, one of the highest points in my country. A place, I like to think, that is closer to God than any ornate edifice that man has built. I came back to the people of Huitupan not because they had left their God but because the God of the Church had left them. They like that I have found ways to weave the God of the mountains, of the clear mountain streams, of the fertile ash-gray soil with the pained and sorrowful God of the Church. I am no longer Catholic, although they do not understand that, since I still baptize the infants, and bless the sacred unions and give comfort to the dying.

But in a larger sense I am catholic, and see all things in the world with purpose, with beginnings and endings, and with connectedness, both good and evil. Some, those functionaries in the church at Chajul, those in the diocese at Huehuetenango, and who knows where else, call me an instrument of the devil. Their very words (but I am not that important). The people of Huitupan know that I am a shaman, only one of several that live in the hills surrounding their village. They call me Father Cota because that is what they want. It does no harm.

This is not my story, but my story to tell, for it is a part of me, a part of my life. What happened to Hector Rabinal, a simple and good man, the son of my sister's cousin, lives on as a rent in my ragged soul. It must be told, not to make the cloth of my soul whole once more, for I am a man, and my soul can be never truly whole, but so that it might never happen again. Or that it might happen again a million times over, but in different ways. Most of this story Hector Rabinal has told me, in letters, in the sacredness of confession, in talks that probed deep into the darkness of the night around us. I will tell Hector Rabinal's story as it must have occurred, as it would have been seen had a god with the eye of an eagle and the wisdom of all the ages been with Hector Rabinal and those he encountered every meter of the way. This, so that some understanding greater than mine alone may enter into the story and make it whole. When I speak of myself it will be as if I am seeing Father Cota as a stranger from a far country, a man whom I hardly know. If I violate Hector's trust in the telling, or distort events out of ignorance, then the God who dwells in all things must be my judge. So be it.

ONE

HECTOR RABINAL straightened from his work and tapped the dirt from one boot with the flat of his machete. The land he stood upon was his. The dirt on his hands, that streaked his trousers and clung to the machete he held, belonged to him as it had belonged to his father and his father's father before him. This was his *finca*, his farm, a small plateau halfway up the trail that wound around Mount Zacapa. The small piece of ground was hardly different from the other dozen or more *fincas* visible from this slope. Everywhere he looked the earth ascended like stairs, terraced again and again, year after year for generations, up and over the rise and fall of land that surrounded him. The only breaks in the terraces were clumps of trees and a few scattered houses and the winding trails that led down into Huitupan, the village that surrounded a small dirt *parque* or plaza that Hector could just see.

From where he stood he gazed over the land of his brothers and his wife Leticia's brothers and of both their cousins, all with fields turned and planted, some with rows of green already waving like small flags in the light breeze. Next to the fields, trees and vines of apples and grapes and peaches swayed in the thin mountain air and filtered light in soft patches across the rich ground. Nearby, bunches of coffee beans hung green and firm on three rows of bushes. Next to them, nearer to his house where Leticia cooked the noon meal and cared for their sons, yellow-green leaves of *frijoles negros* and stiff blades of *maíz* sprouted in the dark soil.

The stream below wound its way beside his land and through the center of Huitupan, where women slapped their bright clothes on the flat rocks, and flowed down to Chajul where it joined the Motagua River as it rushed to the east and then slid into the sea at Puerto Barrios, a place that Hector Rabinal had never been but that he knew because he could read and because he listened closely to what was said. From a young age Father Cota taught Hector Rabinal to calculate liters of beans and kilos of corn, and to read and to write, first in Spanish and then, when he saw how quickly Hector learned, in English. That was more than twenty years before, but Hector still remembered the feeling of magic as his name first appeared black and thick from the end of his pen.

That magic, the way words appear and the way they stand for real things, for people and sky and tears, he wanted Father Cota to teach his sons. Even though Efrán had less than two years, Tomasito was five, and Hector knew that to learn at a young age was the only way to become a man of understanding.

But Father Cota had disappeared, gone as suddenly and silently as smoke in a quick breeze. Father Cota was a man of good impulses and had not been wrong in what he did. To feed the hungry, to give shelter to those who had none, was not wrong. The mistake was not recognizing that he could not — without endangering the whole village of Huitupan — do those things for the weary and ragged bands of men who wandered through the country, either pursuing or, more often, being pursued by the brown-shirted military. Father Cota was not interested in the politics of governments; he thought that the needs of people bowed not to the right or to the left, that there were no just or unjust sides, that the well-being of the people was all that mattered. Those, Father Cota found out, were foolish thoughts, ones that he no longer had. You give aid to the enemy and you become the enemy.

Word had come to Father Cota in the middle of the night that the government soldiers were coming, that he would be taken to the capital, that he was considered a troublemaker, even a traitor. He had time only to take a few of his possessions together with some legal instruments that he had been developing — land titles for the people of Huitupan and so on. With only a few words to Hector Rabinal and no other, he slipped out into the darkness.

That night Father Cota and Hector Rabinal had stood outside under the shadow of the dark sky. They spoke softly in English so that even if someone could hear he would not understand. The leather *cartera* that Father Cota carried was fastened with broad straps and packed so full that he sat on it as he spoke. It was heavy, not with his many belongings, for he had few, but with things of value — his books and, most importantly, the papers that showed the ownership of the land. Papers that at one time, before Hector's dead father was even born, the men from Huitupan had traveled six days to the capital for the president himself to sign. That was long ago, but many years after the great earthquakes had destroyed the old city.

Hector saw no need to worry. "The papers are ours, and the land is ours. Everyone knows that where we stand belongs to me. How could it be the land of some-one else?"

But all along Hector knew. He had heard the rumors. Land had been taken in Presa when the people were accused of helping the rebel soldiers. The priest in Chajul had said it was so. "But who could trust him?" Hector asked. "For a half-hour mass he collects what a poor Indian earns in a month. And unlike you, Father Cota, he would never think to waken us from our igno-rant sleep."

Father Cota shook his head and motioned for Hector to kneel beside him. He told Hector that the papers were no longer safe in Huitupan, that it was not safe for him, that he could be taken away at any time. "But, why?" Hector asked. "Who would take you away?"

Father Cota looked around as if his eyes could penetrate the night. Then he told Hector, "Many in the world are evil; you can no longer know a vulture by its feathers, but only by what it eats." Then Father Cota told him where he would be, at the home of his cousin in the village of Altamirano, a hundred kilometers or more into Mexico. "Tell no one where I have gone," Father Cota said. "You must swear that it will be your secret, for I may not be safe even in Mexico. I am afraid that I have made many enemies."

"How could a man who tries only to do what is right have enemies?" Hector asked.

And Father Cota was as puzzled as Hector and could not answer.

After a moment Hector said, "Mexico. That is not your home. And what good in Mexico are the papers for our land?"

"What good will be a tin of ashes here?" Father Cota asked. "You must trust me."

"With my son's life I would trust you," Hector said.

With that, as if he had only been waiting for those words, Father Cota sprang up as quickly as a young man. He hoisted his load to one shoulder and left without another word.

In a few weeks Hector had called a meeting of the

village men. He was the natural leader since Father Cota was gone and was wise beyond his thirty-four years. The business of Huitupan had to go on. A teacher would have to be found, perhaps more money raised to pay him. The church had a small mission and a school in Chajul, but it was much too far. The bishop had earlier sent word that perhaps those schools outside Chajul, such as the one at Huitupan, would be operated by the government, and that they would hear at the right time, but they must be patient. But for himself, Hector said to all the men, he would not be patient. His sons would grow old while they waited. He would not wait for the church or for the government.

Then Hector told the men that they must guard their land and their homes, that rumors whipped through the mountain valleys, telling how land, even entire villages, had been taken.

While Hector had spoken what words he could at the meeting, his promise of silence to Father Cota hovered over his heart like high clouds of a thunderstorm that grow heavy as they rise above the mountains. Some of the men thought Father Cota might have died at a remote spot on the trail to Presa where his sister lives. Father Cota is no longer a young man, they said. It could have happened. The javelinas would have left no remains. Hector only shook his head and said, no, I know that is not true, and would say no more.

After the meeting Hector's cousin Gabriel warned him not to speak again. "You will disappear like Father Cota," he said, "or you will be driven from your land."

"But we need a school for our children," Hector said. "And besides," he asked, "who is to hear my words? All here are my friends, my family. Who else will speak up? Now that Father Cota is gone they all look to me."

Gabriel had known more than he could tell, but he was afraid. He only shook his head and walked away.

Hector returned to his work in the field, hacking at the tangle of vines that had choked its way around the trunk of an apple tree.

He looked back at his house. He had built it well, secure against the side of Mount Zacapa, on a flat ledge that centuries before had been cleared by a rockslide. The walls were made of thick blocks that Hector had shaped from the mountain's clay and the roof held many layers of thatch to shed the rain while it let the smoke from their fire drift into the sky. Even then, a wisp of dark smoke hung above the roof and from sixty meters away Hector could smell the corn of the tortillas and knew how they darkened on the flat stone. The Ladinos eat *pan*, but men such as Hector, the Indians of Guatemala, must have tortillas of ground corn or be weak.

A cart loaded with barrels and clay pots of water sat next to the house and tilted forward down the trail that led from the stream. Something behind it moved, something larger than a dog, and Hector stopped his work, stretched his back, then stared at the cart. Its wooden handle stood up in the sun like a cross. Hector moved down the hill a few steps toward the house and stopped to look again. He shaded his eyes from the glare and spotted what appeared to be two men kneeling behind the cart. They moved toward the house, not upright like men, but crouched low, almost on all fours as if they were dogs. One held a gun, a rifle, while the other lit a torch of brush. He held it while it caught and burst into flame.

Hector started to move and then froze, unable to take a step, unable to believe that this was happening, as if this were a night of the full moon and he was caught in restless sleep.

Both men wore army fatigues with the outline of a white hand on the back of their shirts. Hector knew of the men of the white hands — they were the takers of the land.

Then Leticia and Tomasito appeared at the doorway. Hector tried to shout, but his voice was silent. In another moment one soldier tossed the torch to the roof and the straw began to burn with smoke that would not rise in the motionless air. Leticia screamed and called Hector's name. She started to run, carrying little Efrán while Tomasito fell behind her and cried out.

Hector's hand tightened around the handle of his machete, and he started across the soft, tilled earth toward the house. He moved, crouching low, losing his hat as he ran. By then — it could only have been two or three minutes — orange flames and black smoke streamed from the roof, then out an open window. One of the soldiers stood. His belly pushed his shirt tight and his rifle was heavy at his shoulder.

Leticia ran back toward the house shielding her face

from the heat. As Hector moved, his feet scarcely felt the dirt beneath them. Then in another moment he was upon the brownshirts. His hand turned to steel as he gripped the machete. The fat standing soldier jerked around and as his eyes found Hector a harsh sound lept from his throat. Hector swung the machete and the soldier's neck was to the blade just one more thick banana stalk, and he fell in two pieces.

Too late his *compañero* heard Hector's roar above that of the dying house, and with another swing of Hector's machete he fell, twisted, slumped against the cart.

Leticia lifted Tomasito by one arm and dragged him with her. Hector's eyes burned from the smoke and heat and the soldiers' blood streaked the white of his shirt. Leticia stopped at the edge of the woods, waiting for him. Hector grabbed a pot of water from the cart and tossed it at the house, but the flames drove him back.

A truck not yet in sight whined in low gear as it struggled up the incline, and Hector motioned to Leticia to move into the woods, to hide. She stared at him for a moment with sadness and anger and fear and helplessness all on her face, a look that Hector could never again remove from his mind. Then Tomasito scrambled past her and the three of them slid into the underbrush, leaving Hector alone with the crack and spew of the crumbling house.

Even before the truck stopped more brown-shirted men tumbled from its canvas back. Hector moved away from what remained of the blazing house toward the orchard and waited on one knee until the soldiers spotted him. Then he stood, defiantly waved the blood-stained machete at them, and quickly raced through the rows of fruit trees that curved up the hill and away from the woods that concealed Leticia and the boys.

The soldiers fired two or three shots and their shouts chased after Hector, but they were slow in their heavy boots and Hector knew that he would be safe, for a while, at least.

As Hector ran he thought of Leticia, the look on her face as she waited at the edge of the woods. Always to him Leticia was young and beautiful, but at that moment he had seen her change, become a woman who had in an instant grown old. Sad and old. A thought Hector could not rid himself of. Not even the fear and anger he felt could erase it.

But Hector knew that Leticia would be safe if she went to Todos Santos, to the home of Adolfo, her brother, who was a good man and knew a priest he could trust — one who would hide them. The mountains fall away from Huitupan to Todos Santos, so the way would be easy. Leticia had gone that way many times and knew it well.

After a half hour of running Hector left the fields behind and entered a dense woods that for centuries had clung to land too rugged to cultivate, a place where he had often gone to gather dead limbs for firewood. There he stopped and listened. Over the quick and harsh sounds of his own breath, Hector could hear shouts from behind and below that echoed faintly through the valley. He moved quickly and silently deep into the woods. There he found a ravine half-filled with dead brush and limbs and leaves. Like a swimmer diving to the depths of a river he worked his way to the bottom of the ravine, being careful not to leave a wake in the brush, covering himself so that he could hardly breathe through the tangle above him.

At first Hector felt buried alive and panic fought against his fear, but he forced himself to lie still.

Just at dark soldiers stomped by, their boots only meters away. Hector's muscles ached to their center and urine had stiffened the legs of his breeches, but he did not move. That night while he prayed, the wind blew from the north and tossed leaves on the ravine like soft rain on a fresh grave.

In a fever Hector dreamed that Leticia had come with a bolt of cloth the color of a sunset and begun to sew a fine suit of clothes for him. Day and night she patterned and cut the cloth, then began sewing the pieces together. But when one piece was sewn and she began another, the first unravelled and she wept but was unable to stop sewing. Leticia grew thin and her fingers bled, but still she sewed, her face covered with her tears.

Then the dryness of Hector's throat awoke him and he started to cry out, not knowing where he was. But his tongue was swollen and silent and thirst drove him from the ravine into a moonless night where a single star fell in a bitter arc.

He stumbled down a rough slope and finally heard the mountain stream. Its water revived him, but the nightmare would not go away. The roar of the stream covered all other sounds of the night and he felt fear for himself and was ashamed of his selfishness. In the dark water he washed his shirt and breeches over and over again, pounding them on the black rocks under his feet. In his mind the stream had turned to red. He shivered. He was cold and afraid.

Although Hector was only a poor *campesino*, his family never before had suffered or been without him. What must he do? To go to them would betray them, but to run and hide was the act of a coward. He had never before known how fear can confuse a man, but at that moment he felt that his heart had been gripped by the black claw of fear.

Then Hector remembered Father Cota, how he had gone to his cousin in Altomirano. Mexico was no more than two days to the west, three days if he went north and bypassed La Mesilla. Father Cota was wise. He would know what Hector should do. Going across the mountains would not be easy, but they were Hector's home. The valley would not be safe — it might never be for him — and he felt a sadness that pushed him to the ground, to his knees. He prayed to his father's God, the God of the mountains, for strength. Then with one last drink of water he climbed up and away from the stream for a hundred meters. He took a moment to study the stars, then turned to the north, the charred smell of his home still hanging in his nostrils. In the dark he scrambled up the steep slope that would lead him to Mexico.

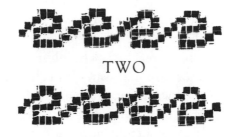

TWO

SOME THINGS a man can tell only to his God — they are for no other to hear — but when blood is smeared across a man's clothes and penetrates to his soul he must have help to cleanse himself. Hector bowed his head; he could not look up as he told Father Cota his story and asked for his help. And then for a long time Hector could only hear Father Cota's shallow breathing, the breathing of an old man while he waited, and Hector found himself wondering why he was there, why he had come to someone feeble when strength was what he needed.

They were alone in a house in the village of Altomirano. Hector sat on the packed dirt of the floor.

The walls, made of earth and poles, soaked up the dim light of candles. A roll of blankets leaned in one corner, and, except for an altar that filled the center of the room, the house was empty. The altar was cave-like, an enclosure, its top made of green branches that lay high across the pole rafters of the room. The sides of the altar were bundles of dried plants that hung tops down in a large circle. The enclosure was as wide as the length of two men and as deep as the length of one. Its top Hector could not have reached. The altar contained a *santo* that Hector only half-saw through the dried branches. It glowed with paint of many colors and stood half the size of a man. San Isidro. In front, guarding the *santo*, stood eight miniature bulls shaped from *barro*, then fired and burnished until they gleamed. Lines of candles rode on the backs of the bulls and layers of melted wax coated them like shiny saddles.

Father Cota had offered Hector food and he had eaten. The empty bowl was beside him, but he had a hunger that *frijoles* could not fill. Hector sat and watched the older man. Now that he had told his story, he felt lighter, and his strength had surged through him once more. He was impatient, but he respected Father Cota, so still he sat and waited. He was a man strange to see in that country, with eyes the color of an overcast sky and hair thin, the color of corn tassels. His lips moved, but he made no sound. His eyes were shut as if they would never open.

Still Hector waited. Sometimes he slept as he sat, but

always the flames and Leticia's face stirred him back awake to the shadowed room.

It had been dark for many hours when Father Cota began to speak. He told Hector that what he had done was not evil in itself, that he had not been wrong to defend his home and his family, but that his soul was tarnished and must be cleansed. He told Hector that he should sleep for a few hours and meet him in the church when it was light. Father Cota then left, saying that he must make things ready, and Hector sat alone with the blackness of the bulls and the flickering of the light. Then he slept.

At first light Hector awakened and found the church. The building was simple, its adobe walls whitewashed, an arch of lapis looped over the door. Already a woman knelt there, moving slowly on her knees to the altar. She chanted softly as she rocked forward on the hard-packed dirt floor, her voice no more than the whimper of a lost child.

The floor of the church was strewn with small branches of pine. The needles slid beneath Hector's feet as he walked. A giant cross, stretching twenty feet or more, leaned against the wall on his left and on his right was another the same size, but wrapped in purple cloth. The church held no pews. Along each wall stood wooden *santos*, taller than any man, each draped with ribbons of every color and adorned with fresh flowers. Hector felt judgment in their stares and tried to fight off the heaviness that descended upon him.

Father Cota had placed candles in a half-circle on

the floor. The candles were of all sizes, some no longer than a small finger and others larger than a boy's arm. They blazed in the gloom of the church. Father Cota stood before them, his head slightly bowed. Hector watched as his lips moved with the rhythm of a chant before it could be heard. The aroma from the candle smoke and the crushed pine needles filled his nostrils. He breathed deeply, hoping to release the weight inside him.

In front of the candles Father Cota had arranged seven eggs in a circle. In the center of the circle he had placed a chicken, its feathers full and red, its feet securely bound. The chicken did not struggle and was strangely silent, though Hector could tell by the glisten of its eye that it was alive.

At the the front of the circle of eggs, a red clay jar was filled with *posh*, a drink that Father Cota had made from the cane of the fields and the juice of many *piñas*, a drink that was strong enough to cleanse any soul.

Father Cota motioned for Hector to come closer, to stand beside him, and then he bent slowly over and took the jar of *posh*, cradling it with both hands. He took a sip and then another and continued his chant. His words were in a tongue that Hector did not know. Then Father Cota passed the jar and Hector drank deeply, welcoming the coolness that was followed by heat. He wanted it to take his mind away, take it to a place where it had been before this nightmare had begun, to wipe his memory clean.

Then Father Cota turned slowly, stopping three

times before he completed a circle. At each stop he
sprinkled the pine boughs with *posh*. He continued to
chant, varying the pitch, changing the rhythm, sipping
the *posh*. Hector drank as Father Cota drank, and the
room began to spin. The chant became Hector's, a part
of him, and he felt it in his soul and in his bones. Father
Cota lifted the pine boughs and swept their stiffness
over Hector's body, letting them rise and fall with the
rhythm of his chant. Then he lifted the chicken and
holding it by the legs brushed Hector's body lightly, taking his darkness with it. Then Father Cota rubbed the
eggs, one at a time, down Hector's arms, across his neck
and forehead, and placed them again on the floor.

Then the chanting stopped. Father Cota raised the
chicken upward, over his head, as if trying to touch it to
the ceiling of the church; then in one quick movement
he brought it down and with a quick twist broke its
neck without drawing blood. He held the bird close
until its last struggle was done. Then he touched its
limp head to the floor of the church and began to chant
again. This time, without a word from Father Cota,
Hector closed his eyes and their voices became one,
their words joined as if from one mouth, one body. The
words were Hector's as if he had learned them while a
young child, as if he had never known another
language.

When Hector opened his eyes Father Cota was no
longer chanting but stood calmly by him, patiently
watching. A smile was on his cracked lips and a look of
peace covered his face. "It is good," he said. "Now let us

eat and drink." They left the church and went to the house of Father Cota's cousin where a table was prepared, already heavy with squash and corn and fruit of many kinds. His cousin's wife had prepared three kinds of tamales, some filled with *frijoles negros*, some with a dark and rich *mole*, and the rest stuffed with the darkened leaves of holy basil that left a sweet and *anis* flavor in Hector's mouth. They ate and they drank. Laughter filled the room and poured from Hector's heart, for now he knew why he had come to Father Cota, and now he understood that strength can come from many places, even from feeble old men. The day was good. They would talk tomorrow.

"What you must do will not be easy." Father Cota spoke quietly, and Hector listened to each word. They were alone again. It was morning and the cleansing and the *posh* and the food and laughter had restored Hector. It was early, the light moved across the room slowly, the shadows of the young day were long. "You could stay here," Father Cota said, "or perhaps go to the camps near the lake, the one north of Frontera Comalapa. Many like you are there."

As he talked he drew circles in the dirt floor, as if each circle might hold what was left of Hector's life. Each of the circles overlapped with another — none was complete in itself. Father Cota had lived for many years and had powers in his soul and in his mind. But even Father Cota could not have all the answers for every man, and he feared the burden of completing what was only partially given. With the circles that always touched he could only try. "But in the camps," he continued, "already there are too many people. They fight over too little food, their children are sick from bad water, the men cannot leave except to work almost as slaves for the owners of the land that joins the camp. They receive the pay, not of men, but of children." He shook his head as he talked, the circles on the ground grew larger. "And who can say? The Mexicans — they don't want our people there — they may force everyone back to Guatemala, but to where? For what? For you that would be impossible. For you there must be more."

Father Cota saw Hector as he would have seen his own son. He had known that from a young age Hector was different from the others, that with his help Hector's vision could be stretched beyond the ancient mountains that surrounded Huitupan. And now Father Cota knew that he had almost lost Hector, and even though he never would have wished for him to suffer this kind of pain, Father Cota saw that moment as the one chance that Hector might have. Out of tragedy and loss something greater could sprout and grow and even flourish.

"I could slip back to Todos Santos," Hector said, "and live with Leticia's brother. He is a good man and can be trusted. Then soon I can go back to Huitupan. The soldiers will forget, the government will change, a judge that is fair would understand and pardon me."

Father Cota stopped him with the wave of his hand. "Not today and not for many months or even years would that be possible. Yes, Leticia's brother is a good man — that I have heard — but he risks all that he has, his land, even his life, by hiding your family. Do you want more blood on your hands?"

Hector did not have to answer. Father Cota reached over and gripped his arm as he spoke, and Hector felt Father Cota's power replacing what he had lost. "Some have gone north, to *Estados Unidos*. There is risk in doing so, and it is many kilometers to travel, but if you are intelligent and careful and willing to work hard, a way can be found to stay." Those were the words of Father Cota, words that he believed to be true or he never would have spoken them, although much later he also saw that the words came from what he wanted, perhaps too badly, to be true.

"But what of Leticia, of my sons?" Hector asked and tried to visualize the United States, California or Texas, the names that he knew, and other, unknown places, cities filled with many cars and televisions and loud music, places where everyone was rich. Places where every man had a tractor with which to work his field.

"When you have money and a safe place to live, after only perhaps a few months, for there is much work there, you can write me a letter here at Altomirano and send money for a bus. Then I will find Leticia and tell her how to find you. After that, *si dios quiere*, you can be together and have a new and safe life in the States." That is what Father Cota said and what he believed to be the best. He could do no more.

"But," Hector asked, "what if you are no longer here, but have gone back to Huitupan, to your house, to your work as our shaman? For you will be needed there."

"Hector," he said, and his voice was gentle and sad, "it is very possible that by now there is no longer the Huitupan that we knew. And besides, my work is where I am. In Huitupan or here, it is all the same. And I am marked the same as you. The blame, my guilt, is as great as yours. To the government my words have cut as deeply as your machete."

Hector had lost his confidence in only a few moments. "But how can I go?" he asked. "What will I tell Leticia? And how? I have no money. I have never before been even this distance from Huitupan. America is too far."

Father Cota gripped both of Hector's wrists and spoke deeply from his heart. "I will send word to Leticia. She must accept your decision and wait for you. She will have to understand, for there can be no other way. Your legs are strong, your mind is quick. You need only know the direction north, and the sun and the stars will tell you that. Until you get farther from Guatemala distrust roads with surfaces that are hard, and no one will stop you. Trust your God and yourself; call on the wisdom that comes from being the son of your father. What little money I have will be yours."

Hector shook his head. "No," was all he could say.

"Everything can be repaid," Father Cota said. "In some way, at some time."

Then Father Cota stood. "Remember to speak the language of Mexico," he said. "You are no longer from

Huitupan, but from Comitan, in the state of Chiapas. Just another poor Mexican headed to the north."

"But how can I cross into America? Is there danger there?"

"When you are close you will find a way. Watch and listen. Remember that you can plan for many things, but finally you must remember to have trust."

Then Father Cota handed Hector a small purse made of leather. He could feel the roll of pesos inside. Then a blanket and a shirt rolled together and tied. Finally a banana leaf, folded and fat with tortillas. Hector took all that he was given. He grasped his machete and slung the bedroll over one shoulder. Without another word he stepped out into the dampness of the morning, glancing at the sun that gleamed through the haze. He felt Father Cota's eyes follow him as he found a trail that led to the north. He did not look back.

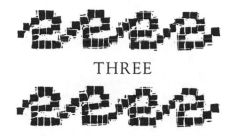

THREE

HECTOR stopped in the village that is called Peregrina. To get there he had traveled two thousand kilometers north of his home. On his journey he had learned but one thing. The dispossessed souls of the earth, the *campesinos*, the poor, will share from what little they have more readily than the rich will share from their abundance.

His shame and his guilt were hard to bear. Many nights he had watched the stars move across the sky, then lifted himself off the dirt that was his bed and turned to face the south, where the same stars, the ones that guided him to that place, hung above the ash of his home. On one of those lonely nights the knowledge came to him that he might never return to Huitupan, at least not for many years, perhaps never. That thought burned across his heart, then died like a falling star. He was strong and young and not afraid, but still his tears splattered in the black dust of the night and he cursed the God of the mountains. Much later Hector would see that his God had not left him, but that he had left his God.

But to return to Huitupan now would help no one. And to have come that far, to be at that place in the middle of an immense desert, had not been without cost. Two men had died at his hand. He said that aloud in the night, a whisper to himself, and the words swirled about him like a rain-swollen river. At that moment he swore an oath. "I will never kill another man. For me to die would hold less pain."

To get there he had begged, and yes, he had stolen, but only food, nothing else, and food belonged to the earth and the chance of sun and rain and could be claimed by no man but for the good fortune of passing his days at a certain place. And that could change.

The farther to the north he traveled, the more he lost himself. Near the border, when first he slipped into Mexico, men could see that he was from the mountains near Chajul, as if he were still wrapped in the placenta of his birthplace. But there, in Peregrina, those few who noticed found him to be just another Chiapan or Oaxacan wandering north.

That day in Peregrina was the same as the dozen or more days that stretched before it. The men moved into the desert as it became light, and Hector went with them. They were silent; the thin bray of one ragged burro broke the quiet, a complaint against the weight it carried, the water necessary for twenty men.

They cut *maguey* with machetes and flat-headed steel poles, slicing and prying it loose from the sand. They trimmed the broad, tough leaves until the stack of *maguey* looked like a pile of giant *piñas*. Hector's hands bore the cuts and slices from the leaves, but he did not care. He had once again found the pleasure of working day after day, finding an old rhythm within himself that had been lost.

The men talked little. There was no laughter — to laugh took strength, to open one's mouth in the heat was to lose precious water.

When the sun was high they cut *nopales*, trimming their spines. The young leaves when peeled were tender and slippery like the flesh of mangoes, but without the sweetness. Hector ate, but emptiness was always with him; his hunger never left. Like the others he pushed four stalks of the *maguey* into the ground, and over them spread his shirt for a little shade, a place to rest a few minutes on the hot sand. Sometimes in his half-sleep he saw the mountains or smelled the scorched corn of Leticia's tortillas in the still air, but neither was there.

The men sharpened their machetes on stones of sand, and by evening great piles of cactus wound across the flatness. Then they became like burros loaded with the day's harvest. Hector watched his shadow as he walked. It was bent and monstrous. The hump of his spiny load loomed larger than the man.

The days at Peregrina could not be longer than those days at Huitupan, but the sun beat down with anger and rain did not fall. There were no trees for fruit and the *maíz* had ears no larger than green bananas. The people were poor and pay was only enough for a little beans or rice and some days a little milk to stir with the *nopales* that he had cut. Hector had to save for his journey to the north, to Texas, a place where he knew there was much money to be earned — enough for Leticia and his sons to join him, enough for them to ride the bus the entire distance. Hector knew that it would happen, perhaps in only a few months or even in a few weeks. In the *Estados Unidos* who could say how quickly it might be, for Hector had sworn to work very hard in that place where everyone could become rich.

The bus from the south stopped at Peregrina once a day, and the young women watched until it was gone. But no one could leave without money. The people of Peregrina were not like Hector. They were at their home. Where else could they know to go?

There, lives had a pattern. When the men did not cut the *maguey* they trained their *peregrinas*, their falcons, captured when they were young, to catch *cascabeles*, the large snakes with rattles. The meat when boiled in goat's milk was white and sweet, and the women stretched and dried the skins on woven limbs and sold them by the side of the great highway that came near the village. The women danced and waved the dried skins at the passing cars. Beside them, in cages of sticks bound with fibers of the *maguey*, were the falcons, prizes for the lucky traveler with a few pesos.

It was a Sunday. Hector watched the women by the side of the road. They whirled and danced, dry and frail, like husks caught in a whirlwind. Hundreds of cars passed along the highway, for it was important that many journey from the capital to Monterrey and then back. Trucks from San Luis Potosi came each Sunday — they would come later that day — for the *maguey* which by then was a stack twenty paces across and higher than two men. Enough to make many barrels of mescal or even tequila.

The men were happy, for today they would be paid. Hector squatted in the narrow shade of the stacked *maguey* with Rafael. Hector felt comfortable with him because he asked few questions.

Hector stayed in the house of Rafael's uncle who was away and might not return. No one knew, or no one would say. The house had one room. Hector's hat brushed its ceiling when he stood, and the door was only a flap of dried cactus, flattened and tied. Its wall on the east was made of tin, old and from another building, and in the mornings narrow points of light angled in through rusted nail holes and across the room like those in portraits of the saints. It was not Hector's home, but he was grateful.

Rafael was the mayor of Peregrina and in his patience and silence there was much to be learned. He and

Hector sipped *pulque* from red cups made of the desert's clay.

"At our fiestas," Rafael said, "we break the cups when they are empty." And he made a gesture as if to throw the cup to the ground. "You must stay for that. We drink much *pulque*, roast three, even four young goats, we dance, we laugh, the women are beautiful."

For a moment Hector didn't answer. A fiesta was not possible in that place, it seemed. But Rafael had been kind, taking Hector in from the desert where he wandered, giving him shelter and work, so he nodded. "Yes, a fiesta would be fine. You are very gracious. But you know I am on the way to the north and must continue. Perhaps even in the morning, after I am paid, I will go."

Rafael ignored what he said. "Soon it will be time for my daughter, Elena, to have a husband, a house of her own, probably that of my uncle, the one that is now yours."

Elena was waving the dried snake skins at the passing cars. She had the body of a child; her breasts could not hold enough milk for an infant. But her face was that of a woman, one that was pretty, but only for a brief time, for already Hector could see the old woman's marks and creases that came quickly in this place.

They watched the women, and Hector listened to Rafael without looking at his face. "Many men come through Peregrina on their way to the north," he said. "Only a few stop for more than a day. All are desperate in some way: to start a new life, for the opportunity to work, for the magic dollar of the north. But some, and you are one, journey to leave the darkness that follows them, that will be with them even when they cross the Rio Grande and lose themselves in one of the great cities. You carry your story in your eyes."

Hector started to interrupt, to protest, but Rafael shook his head to silence him.

"Do not explain," he said. "There is no need for me to know your story, for you are an honorable man. That, also, shows in your eyes. But I must tell you that if you are caught, whether crossing the river or miles to the north, the authorities will know that you are not from this country, that you are from another place that lies to the south, and they will send you back. You are not the first that I have seen."

Then Rafael spoke again, nodding his head toward Elena. "If you will stay, a house and work will be yours — perhaps a wife. This place to stop is as good as you will find to the north. The ways up there are restless, and there is no peace to be found."

Hector could not answer aloud. He looked at the ground and shook his head.

"Stay here," Rafael said and moved to his house, disappearing inside.

Hector felt a strong need to run, to leave, but Rafael's quiet power held him there and he remained squatting in the shade of the stack of *maguey*, no longer seeing the women or the flash of traffic on the shimmer of the highway. But over and over again he repeated Rafael's words to himself. "The authorities will know that you are not from this country . . . they will send you back . . . they will send you back." Was it the way he looked? Some mark upon his face? The way he talked? How could he know. He felt as he had always been and that could not be changed — not in a few weeks.

Perhaps Rafael was right. One place might be as good as another. For Hector there might never be another place that was his and was safe.

Then Rafael was beside him again. "Listen carefully," he said, and handed Hector a small cloth folded over a stack of tortillas. Then he held out a tobacco pouch that was heavy with coins and put it in his hand. Hector started to object, but Rafael stopped him.

"I know you must go. In the morning," he said. "Just as it is light the bus will stop if you are at the side of the road. It is a long journey to the north. The bus will go through Saltillo, then on to Monterrey, a city of many people. One hundred and sixty kilometers north of Monterrey the bus will stop at the pueblo of La Gloria, but only for a few minutes. That is where you get off. It is important. Farther north is the *Inspección Federal* and although they might not detain you, the risk is too great. At La Gloria replenish your water and follow the Rio Salado to the northwest, perhaps fifty kilometers, until you find a railroad track." With a stick Rafael drew a line in the sand. "If you follow the tracks north you will come to a camp at the edge of Nuevo Laredo where many others such as you have come to stay before they cross the river. Do you understand?"

Hector had listened carefully, and although the country was strange to him, he could remember the way as if it were drawn onto a map in his head. "Yes," he said, "I must go."

"How can I repay you?" Hector asked, holding up the purse of coins. He knew that if his father were alive he would be filled with shame — his son accepting money that had not been earned. But this was not his father's time.

Rafael shook his head and began to speak. "Once, when I was young I took money that was not mine. More than once I did this, traveling from one city to the next. I knew better but was impatient with the world. For months I was gone from Peregrina. This, as I say, occurred many years ago, when I was young, before I had a wife of my own. The authorities never caught me, and my pockets became fat with pesos. I thought myself to be very important.

"With part of the money I bought an expensive *rebo-zo*, woven with threads of every color, a present for my mother. But the gift was not from my heart, although I loved her greatly, but was an act of arrogance, a way of showing my father and the others of this poor village how rich I had become."

He looked out at the highway and sighed. "I stepped off the bus in my fine clothes, in my new boots, carrying the *rebozo* so everyone could see, and walked to my father's house, just over there." And he pointed across the way. His voice was low, and at that moment Hector listened to him as if Rafael were the only person on the earth. "My father met me at the door. He told me that my mother had died three weeks before, that she had asked for me with her last breath. Where have you been? my father asked. I held the *rebozo* out and he spit upon it.

"You ask how you can repay me? For you there will be many ways. Some will not require money. You will know when the time is right. When it happens, if you think of me, I will be repaid. Perhaps in time my penance will be enough."

Rafael then shook Hector's hand, wished him good health, and walked away. The next morning Hector would go north again, each mile taking him farther away, yet, he prayed, closer.

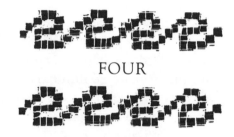

FOUR

TO EAT TORTILLAS while riding on a fine bus softens the memory and pain of walking. Hector had taken a seat on the right side of the bus so that he could read the signs. La Gloria. The most important sign would be La Gloria. For miles there were none that he recognized, none that Rafael said that he would see. The bus stopped often, and by the time the mountains rose small and dim from the desert the bus was crowded with many others who had begun their journeys.

Hector rode with his head against the window, which opened only a crack, and tried to keep his eyes open for the signs, but it was not always possible. His head

37

bounced quietly on the window but did not keep him from falling into a half-sleep. His mind drifted to a place where it could find no rest.

He dreamed of Huitupan, of the cemetery that held the graves of his father and mother, the crosses and flowers and painted stones that lined the graves. The men in brown shirts were there, shoveling, uncovering their graves. They pulled the caskets out and spit on them. The wood was like new. When they opened his father's casket he was still alive, but very frail, and they prodded him with the butts of their guns to make him run, but he couldn't. Hector stood there and watched, although for some reason the soldiers could not see him. But his father could. He was dressed in his only suit and his eyes were pleading for Hector to help. Hector tried to move toward him and began to take steps, but for some reason he could get no closer. He cried out for the soldiers to stop, but they could not hear him. His father's pleading turned to frustration and then to anger, but still Hector could not move. The soldiers picked his father up and forced him face down into the grave. They shoveled and kicked dirt on him as he screamed. Finally he was silent.

Hector was jolted awake when the driver braked hard and the bus swayed uncertainly. They were curving through mountains made of splintered rock which bore no trees and had no water. Saltillo. The sign flashed like a signal in his head.

The city was strange, the hills as barren as the cobblestone streets. Never had he seen a city of so many people with so little that was green.

The driver said they had ten minutes and left the bus. With a short wooden stick, smooth like the handle of a hoe, he walked around the bus and hit each tire. Poing, poing, poing, poing. Hector felt the vibration in his feet and in his head which still rested against the window.

What if the brakes should fail, or a tire blew out and the bus tumbled over the side of a cliff? He could die, and Leticia would never know. But it would be worse to live, to be injured, maybe crippled, to be alone and suffering.

But those were the thoughts of a coward, and he pushed them from his mind. They were unworthy of Hector Rabinal, who was brave, who would go to the north and find a way, with the help of God, to bring his family together once more. He swore that he would.

A young man sat beside him just as the bus started. He talked of many things that Hector did not know. When he should talk of work or his family he talked of games and those who play them in America. That, and of the music from his radio, which Hector had heard and knew, for he, too, had a radio. Before the fire. But the young man pretended that the music was different, as if it were his alone and not the same that Hector had heard.

In the distance to the east a huge city waited, buried in the smoke of buses and cars and factories. The bus took most of an hour to find the city's center. They stopped but for a few minutes and the young man left without an *adiós*. As the bus started he jumped back on carrying a tall bottle of orange drink and his radio. Hector pretended to sleep, but the young man would not stop talking. At least he asked no questions, having no need of answers.

When the bus stopped at La Gloria, Hector stepped onto the hot, dry ground. The long ride had made him stiff and he moved slowly through the town searching for the market. He was in no hurry to face the desert again, to find the route up the Rio Salado, to the train tracks that led north to Nuevo Laredo and the border. He could have ridden forever on the bus if he would have had no dreams.

For a few pesos he filled his sack with tortillas and a small piece of beef that had been dried in the sun. He found a plastic jug in a pile of trash and filled it with cool water.

In the shade of a building near the edge of town he laid out his possessions: a small blanket, his machete, one shirt rolled into a small bundle, the sack of food and the water. That, and the hat on his head, the clothes that he wore, was all.

He secured everything but the water jug in his blanket, then rolled it tightly with a rope, leaving a loop that fit snugly around his shoulder. The handle of the machete stuck out one end where it could be easily grasped. He tied the plastic jug to a belt loop, but after a few steps saw that it was too heavy and slung it over his shoulder.

Hector saw himself as others must, a poor *campesino*, simply another man who was wandering to the north. But he would not be a poor man forever. One day he would reclaim his land. It would be there always and he would return.

A boy riding a bicycle led him to the Rio Salado. The boy had clipped stiff cardboard on the frame of his wheel that went ta-ta-ta-ta against the spokes when he pedaled. He pointed down the dry river bed to the west and then left, racing back to town in a whirr of noise. He was very proud. Hector thought that someday Efrán would have a bicycle and ride in the same way. Yes, it will happen, he said. He knew that he must keep saying that it would.

The Rio Salado lay flat and wide and clear of brush so the way was easy. If it would have had even a hole of water Hector would have bathed, but he had learned not to wish things to be different, for different was not always better.

In only a few minutes La Gloria faded behind him — the noise of the trucks that slowed for the *topes* at the edge of town, the smell of diesel, then that of lard sizzling around the *mercado*, the shrill cries of children as they kicked a can on the streets, and the quiet midday cluck of a few hens chasing grasshoppers across a dusty yard. He left them all.

The monotony of walking a long distance can be comforting, knowing that you will not arrive soon no matter how great the effort, that the distance will be measured in hours or days and not in minutes. So

Hector fell into a pace he could sustain an entire day, or even into the night if necessary. He walked with his head down. An occasional hawk flew over, and he watched its shadow flutter across the sand. There were footprints, dim from the constant wind, but whether from that day or a week before he could not tell, for there had been no rain. A few lizards bobbed their heads as he passed, their throats pink and pulsing. But for many kilometers, until the sun lengthened the shadows of the rocks, he was lost in silence, in the welcome blankness of his mind.

Hector stopped in the shade of a white barked tree that somehow had survived with its roots deep in the sand, down to the river that still ran underground. He took only a few sips of water, saving the little that was left. He tore off a piece of tortilla and chewed slowly. The railroad should be near, but he had seen no sign. If it crossed the river he would find it. He thought back over Rafael's directions step by step and could see no way he could have gone wrong.

He slung his pack over his shoulder and started again, this time the water bottle swung lightly against his hips as he walked, gently prodding him along. He rounded a bend in the river and suddenly stopped, his eye going to something in the shade of a stone ledge. It was a man, perhaps dead, but he saw no vultures around. Hector instinctively reached across his shoulder for the machete and held its familiar handle as he took a few steps closer. Then he let go. The man was old. It was he who should be wary, but he slept as though in his own bed. Hector started to pass by but stopped and stepped closer.

"Old man," he said, looking around to see if anyone else could be there, watching. Perhaps it was a trick. "Old man," he repeated, this time louder and again his hand went to his machete. To Hector, his own voice echoed through the shallow canyon like that of a stranger.

The old man was not startled, but awoke with a smile on his face, as if Hector were his son and he had been waiting for him to pass that way.

He scrambled to his feet and asked, "You are going to Texas, maybe?"

Without waiting for Hector to answer, he said, "That is good. We will travel together, for I have been there many times. Even to Chicago where my youngest son now lives. They pay him much money to cook. He is a very fine cook. He makes deep-dish pizza. I like it very much. Do you?"

Hector shook his head, not knowing what to say, but then told him, yes, he was going to Texas, for work, and then how he would send for his family.

The old man's name was Lupe, and he lived in San Luis Potosi with his wife and daughter, an unfortunate girl who had been sick much of her life and had never married. They ran a tiny store in the front room of their house, but Lupe no longer worked, leaving the buying and selling to the women in his family. His five sons all had moved over the years to the United States and every month sent him money, not very much, but enough to save for his trips.

"Now I will go to see them again. I go every year, to Texas, then to Denver, and then to Chicago."

When he talked Hector could see that his top middle teeth were missing, but his eyes were quick and held no secrets.

"How far is the railroad?" Hector asked. "The one that goes to the north, to Nuevo Laredo."

"The railroad? It is there," and he laughed, pointing to the west.

A trestle spanned the empty river not a hundred meters away. Hector laughed also, glad to have come that far and happy to have Lupe as a companion. He offered some water, and Lupe drank it eagerly. His ancient water jug leaked so he had planned to wait and move on to Nuevo Laredo in the cool of the night. But with water he was ready to continue.

From his belongings Lupe pulled a plastic sack and reached around in it until he found a taco, wrapped in newspaper, fat with meat and beans. He tore it in two and offered half to Hector. Lupe caught the grease that dripped from the taco and rubbed it into the backs of his hands. He motioned to the sun and said that he had the skin that all old men have. But he said it with a laugh, as if to dismiss it as one of life's minor annoyances. Then he took off at a brisk pace, leading the way.

The camp that Rafael had described lay to the west of Nuevo Laredo, not far from the Rio Grande, next to a great pit where trucks came loaded with garbage from early to late. Hector had been there for a day, watching and waiting while Lupe rested, and never before had he seen so much of so little use. Women and children followed and searched through the mounds that the trucks dumped deep from their groaning bowels, desperate for a little food, a scrap of clothing. Boys probed for empty bottles or cans that they sold.

They had come to that barren place, a place to gather, hoping to become invisible for the crossing of the river. All dreamed their own dreams, ones with the strength to carry them for fifty or fifteen hundred kilometers. But dreams can betray you, can be false. A place to gather before the silent move across the river had become for many a place to stay. Some became trapped, unable to go forward, unable to return. Wives and children were abandoned, a man came down with a fever, a child died, the hope for the correct paper from the authorities never quite faded. The reasons to stay were many. Perhaps some became exhausted from their journeys or were beaten down by the heat or by their hunger. Others became discouraged by the odor of decay and death that hovered in the air.

All of that showed on their faces, spoke in the sad way they moved. For two thousand kilometers that place had formed in Hector's mind, taken shape from the stories that he had heard. Before he came and saw with his own eyes the camp had always been a place that held only promises. Now he was not sure.

What the people called their homes were exhausted shacks of many colors, built with scraps of cardboard and tin and even flattened cans, wilted by the sun until they were near collapse. The source of water, one lone spigot, leaned next to a store a thousand meters away. The constant flow of men and women struggling back and forth, bent with the weight of bottles and buckets, left a trail of dust that hung constantly in the heat.

Lupe and Hector squatted next to their packs in the shade of a rusted pickup and watched the hopeless movements of the people.

Finally Hector spoke. "We will not stay here," he said to Lupe. "My dog would not stay here, it is fit only for pigs. Let's move on to the river. We can cross tonight."

"You do not understand, my friend," Lupe said, shaking his head. "I have done this many times, and it is simple if you have a plan. But to make a plan we must stay here for two nights and listen."

"For what?" Hector asked. "In one hour I can find what you need to know — where to cross, what time of night — it cannot be that difficult." He said those words with impatience, for he had come so far and from that very spot he could see the trees that bordered the river.

"Do you want to go to Queretaro or Zacatecas? If we are caught that is where they take us. Five hundred, even a thousand kilometers to the south." And he pointed his bony arm in that direction, away from the river. Lupe's voice shook as he talked. "Then we are not two days crossing the river, but two weeks or two months. Perhaps I would not even try again."

A man approached them. He was thin without looking hungry. His clothes were old but not worn. Lupe pulled his pack over and sat on it.

"Where do you come from?" the man asked.

Hector looked at Lupe, but the old man did not answer and kept his eyes on the ground.

"The south," Hector said. "A long way."

"You are going to Texas?" he asked but didn't wait for an answer. "It is not possible anymore. Not without help." He squatted beside them, trying to look Lupe in the eye, but the old man stared at two boys kicking a can back and forth in the dirt street.

"For a few pesos I guarantee it though. Six hundred. What you make in a few days in Texas. Guaranteed."

Six hundred pesos! Hector thought he could never make that much, not there. Maybe in Texas, but if he were in Texas then the money would not be for that man.

Finally Lupe said, "We don't have the money." Then he looked straight over at the man. "And if we did, we would spend a dozen nights with the señoritas and not waste it on dog turd such as you."

The man turned to Hector, then back to Lupe and jerked himself up. Then with a quick kick of his boot he sprayed dirt in Lupe's face.

Hector did not understand. Lupe struggled to his feet, but the man pushed him and he sprawled backwards across his pack, losing his hat.

Hector felt his fists clench and he moved toward the younger man who in one quick move slid a knife from his boot. Hector thought of his machete, still on the ground behind him, wrapped in the bundle, its black handle ready for his grasp. But he remembered his promise not to raise it in anger again.

"He is an old man," Hector said. "We have no money."

"I cut his balls out," the man said. His eyes were bright and eager. "Then he will forget about the girls. But why bother? His prick is old and withered, anyway."

"You won't live long enough for yours to wither, you son of a bitch dog," Lupe snarled, still on the ground.

Perhaps when you are old you are no longer afraid, Hector thought. Or perhaps Lupe was crazy.

"Shit," the man said and slashed the air with his knife. "The border patrol get you first thing." He slipped the knife back into his boot and started to back away. "I tell them to watch for you. They are my *amigos*, I buy them *cervezas* every night in the hotel bar, in Texas. Yes, I will tell them to watch for a stupid old pig of a man and a coward from the south."

Again Hector thought of his machete. The man had insulted him as no other man had ever dared. But to fight was to risk arrest, and that would end his dream, maybe forever. So he forced himself to stand and not move, his hands at his side, while the man arrogantly strode away.

Hector expected Lupe to be angry with him, for he had only stood by and watched. But who was the man to Hector? Only a stranger who had done him no harm except with words. Hector kept staring where the man had disappeared into the jumble of huts. Then Lupe began to laugh with the cackle of an old man, and Hector turned to see him grinning.

"It is so much easier to be old," he said. "I insult a young man who deserves it, and it is so satisfying. All I get is a little shove. A younger man would have lost his testicles for sure."

"I'm sorry I did not help," Hector said. "Let me explain."

But Lupe stopped him with the wave of his hand. "No," he said. "You were very wise. Who knows who his friends might be?" And with the question he drew his hand flat across his throat, as if it were a knife. "We have not come here to fight — that a man can do closer to his home — even with his wife."

He laughed again, a sound that Hector had come to expect, one that lightened his heart each time he heard it.

"No," Lupe said, "we are here for one reason only — to find the safest way across the river. That is all."

He started to rise and Hector offered him his hand, but he ignored it. He dusted himself off, and they moved away, Lupe leading the way again, bent under the weight of his pack. He was looking for something or someone. The shelters and houses were in rows that resembled those in villages, with streets winding in and out in no certain pattern. But there was no center. Each crossroad was like the one before and at each one Lupe stopped a few moments and listened.

"A vendor I know comes here twice a day selling tortillas from his mother's *tortilleria* in town. He knows everything. We will watch for him." Lupe looked at his watch with its wide silver band and then at the sun as if not trusting what he had seen.

"Let's sit here," he said and dropped his pack to the ground in the shade next to a house. Hector sat on a smooth rock and leaned against a tilted wall that moved with his weight.

"We can walk all afternoon and not find him," Lupe said, "or we wait here and he comes to us."

He looked at Hector as if the choice were his, but Hector trusted the old man and, besides, his boots were worn thin and the heat of the sand had blistered the soles of his feet. "This is good," was all that Hector said.

A woman looked out through an opening which had no door and stared at them suspiciously. Lupe nodded a greeting and with a grin wished her a good afternoon. He spoke to her with a bell in his voice, the way a young man speaks to a señorita. The woman scowled and pulled her head back into the dark of the house.

Lupe leaned his head back and soon was asleep, but the heat and the flies kept Hector on edge. Or perhaps his heart still raced from seeing the flash of the knife. The wind whirled paper and empty cartons and plastic wrappers down the street. They hung on rocks or up against a pole, then blew farther on and collected in a corner where two buildings met. There they rose and fell with the wind before finally settling into their places where they were soon covered by more of the trash that floated and skimmed through the ragged streets.

It was as Lupe said. In less than an hour they heard

the jingle of bells and a man appeared around the corner riding a bicycle. A skinny yellow dog followed him. But it was only the back half of a bicycle that the man rode. In place of the usual front wheel sat a wooden box, painted white and balanced above a tiny wheel, perhaps one from a child's toy. "Rosa's Tortillas" was written in red across the box and a string of bells hung suspended above the handlebars. When the vendor pedaled, the bells jingled with an inviting sound.

The young man, whose name was Rubén, stopped when he saw Lupe. For a moment he said nothing, just grinned and shook his head in disbelief.

"Don Lupe," he said. "You are here again. It must be time for the wealthy to vacation. I thought you had died in the desert and the buzzards had picked your bones."

"Buzzards are too ignorant to bother me," Lupe said. "When I move they know I am alive, but when I am still they are not sure." He gave Rubén his cackle of a laugh and then rose and shook hands with the younger man. Then he dug into his pocket and held out some coins. "Some tortillas, *por favor*," he said, "with my compliments to your beautiful mother."

Rubén flipped open a door of the box and reached in. "For you and your friend, tortillas with *my* compliments." He wrapped the tortillas in brown paper and handed the package to Lupe with a little bow.

Lupe shook his head. "That is good, but it is bad luck to accept your gift. Your generosity will tempt us to stay and our destination is many miles to the north."

Rubén shrugged and accepted the money. "Then perhaps I can help in some other way," he said. He glanced around, waiting until two young men passed, and their quarreling grew faint. Then he leaned toward Hector and Lupe and spoke just above a whisper.

"Go to the west with the river, a half day's walk. You will pass a house that burned and find a ravine that is red with clay. Follow it to the edge of the river and you will find many willows. Cross two hours before the sun is up, find a place to hide, a place where there are no roads. Cover a cloth — your blanket perhaps — with sand and sleep under it until dark. Then move west and north where another river joins the Rio Grande. Follow it. Move only at night. Do you understand?"

Lupe nodded. "There are problems?" he asked. "Never before have I done this. Not in all my years."

"It is different now. You see this?" Rubén waved his arm around. "All is new, not because it is the place these people choose to live, but because the Americans have many men and helicopters and dogs. It is no longer easy. It is no longer safe."

"Why not cross early in the night and move quickly to the north?" Hector asked. "In eight hours we could be many kilometers into Texas."

"That is true," Rubén answered. "But both you and the border patrol have the same thoughts. Listen to what the coyotes say and that is what you will hear. If you pay an honest one," and he shook his head, "he will take you the same way that I have told you. Remember, move only at night."

"We will do as you say." Lupe's voice was soft. "Tomorrow night, or perhaps even tonight."

Hector nodded, yes. He was eager to go. Tomorrow he would be in Texas. It was hard to believe.

Rubén wished them good luck and rode off down the street, the bells jingling even after he had turned the corner and was out of sight.

Lupe stared for a long time at Hector's pack. Finally Hector asked, "What is wrong? Is there something that you need?"

Lupe reached down and drew Hector's machete from the bundle. "This you cannot take across the river." He turned it from side to side and the blade gleamed in the last sun of the day. Hector could not help but look for the red stain of blood.

"I will not go without it," he replied and took it from Lupe's hand. "Today I would not be here except for this. You cannot understand. "

"Yes," Lupe said, "there are many things I cannot understand. But if we go together you must not take this machete." He waited a moment, but Hector was silent. Then Lupe asked, "How many gringos in Texas carry machetes when they walk? How many? What do you think?"

Hector tried to visualize the men in Texas, the way they might move back and forth at the sides of the roads, but nothing appeared.

Lupe shook his head. "Never have I seen even one man carry a machete. To cut trees they use machines," and he swept both hands across and made a noise —

brrrrt. "Why would they need a machete? The border patrol sees a man carrying one of these and he knows he has a Mexican — a stupid Mexican. The buses come back filled with them every day."

But Lupe understood the frustration that showed on Hector's face. "Don't worry," he said. "A machete is easy to sell in Mexico, in a city like this," and he pointed to Nuevo Laredo where already the lights were sparkling against the last pink of the sky. "We will take a bus to town and sell your machete, then find a cool cantina and drink *cervezas*. At the market we will buy some beans to go with our tortillas, perhaps even a little meat, to give us strength, and a sack of oranges. You have some pesos?" he asked and Hector nodded yes. "After we leave the market we will exchange them for American dollars. Then it will be time to return here and start to the river." Lupe said that all in one breath, not giving Hector time to interrupt or to object. Then he added, "Do you agree?"

What could Hector say? He could move faster without Lupe, but if he were seen, his legs could not move fast enough. For once Hector's heart and his mind felt the same and he said yes, the plan is good. Lupe turned to lead the way to town and without hesitation Hector followed.

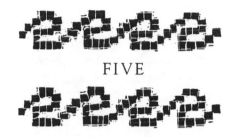

FIVE

HECTOR AND LUPE crossed the Rio Grande before the east was touched with light and slept under a thick sheet of sand in a grove of willows. They burrowed deep like animals to find the coolness and slept all day. They meandered north all that night, following a river bank, groping their way farther from the border.

It had been gray light almost an hour when they dropped their packs to rest. Lupe pointed up the river, to its source, as if by stretching he could reach it.

"This is our river," he said. "We will follow it to the north for many days to where it joins with another, much wider river, the Nueces. Then we will be near —

only one day's walk from the dairy where my son Emilio works. It is not difficult to find, for there the river makes a great bend." His arm traced an arc in the air as he spoke, the motion almost completing a circle.

They carried their packs with one hand, knowing without talking that they would walk only until they found a still pool, a place where the river curved gently and had cut out a hole from the sandy bank. It did not take long. A gravel bar stuck out of the river like the switchback of a mountain road, and there they made their camp. They gathered bundles of stiff grass from the soft river bank and spread them evenly to soften their beds.

Hector pulled off his boots and left them by his pack, then moved the few steps to the river's edge and stripped his clothes from his body, shaking the sand from them. Then he eased into the slight circular drift of shallow water, still cool from the night air. He floated face down, then turned on his back as Lupe splashed out like a small boy to join him.

It was not the stream at Huitupan, but when Hector floated quietly on the surface he saw through his closed eyes the women of his village on their knees at the water's edge, slapping blouses and breeches on the slick rocks. Then Leticia slipped through the water to join him, her smooth hair free from its braid. She laughed, the water splashed, silver drops glistened across her breasts, sparkled in the mat between her legs. Hector felt himself grow stiff until he ached. He turned once more to hide his swollen penis and swam angrily to the center of the river where he floated downstream finding a moment of relief out of Lupe's sight.

Later they washed their clothes and then dressed again right away, the wetness of the cloth a barrier to the heat that had begun to settle around the river's edge. They made no fire but were content to eat a little of what they carried. Hector was in Texas for the second day, and a deep sleep easily overtook him. The hours swept past without dreams.

After two days Lupe felt the danger of being stopped had lessened and they began to travel by day, moving much faster. Hector followed Lupe as he kept steadily to the river bed. Even by day the way was slow. They followed the endless curves, crouching to move under limbs that swept the bank. The deep sand pulled at their boots. But they stayed low in the bed of the river, the only way to be safe.

As they walked they made their own trail, their tracks mixing with the crisscross tracks of birds and deer and small splay-toed creatures. They spotted the smooth curves of snake bellies in the sand and heard their dry rattles. Without speaking they circled around and left them to their solitary places. The horizon was empty and for many hours they moved in silence as if they were the last men to walk upon the earth.

Later in the day Lupe asked Hector if he could speak in English, that the language was necessary in Texas. Hector replied "a little," then said "halloween," and "cowboys," and "sandwich" and was proud.

"I will teach you more," Lupe said, "while we travel

north. When I was a young man I worked in El Moderno, the finest restaurant in my city. I was a fine waiter." And he stopped a moment and pulled himself erect. "My suit was black like this water on a moonless night. The best waiter in San Luis Potosi — everyone would tell you — for eighteen years, until I saved enough to have my own store. Many gringos traveling to Mexico stopped for the fine meals. From them I learned to speak much English. I speak English very good. What I know I have taught my sons and now I will teach you."

Soon the emptiness of the desert was filled with their words. "My name is Hector Rabinal. What is your name? Do you have work? Thank you very much." Then a whole string of wants: "I want boots, please. I want to eat. I want one beer, please." And on and on, step after step. The words Hector had learned from Father Cota began to spring back, awake in his mind where they had slept for so many years.

Just at dusk on the fourth night they came upon the adobe walls of what once must have been a grand house, a place where the trace of an old road crossed the shallows of the river. They made camp in the shelter of one solid wall that still stood, and Hector spent the last minutes of light walking through the crumble of ruins. Nothing of value was left: some broken jars, a few dried pieces of boards with nails now loose in their holes, some rusted horseshoes. Hector thought of his house, the way it must be blackened ashes. Could Leticia's brothers have rebuilt it? He tried to picture it new again, but could only see it burning, the flames reflected in Leticia's eyes.

That night, before sleep overtook him, he tried to imagine who might have lived in that place, the immense work it took to build such a house from the clay of the earth, whether there were women and children, and where they had gone. It all seemed so futile — the endless work, the dreams of men. The sky stretched over him forever, and somewhere he knew his sons might be watching the same stars. He gazed into the wash of white that streaked through the blackness of the night and felt himself sinking, falling forever, before his eyes finally closed in sleep.

On the fifth day Lupe occasionally stopped and moved up the river bank, scanning an abandoned field that bordered the river. A covey of quail rose with a whirr a short distance off, then lit again. They fussed at Lupe before he clambered back down with a grin.

"We will stop here," he said, "for a small siesta."

Hector was grateful for a rest and sat with his back to a sapling, the sun splattering down through its leaves.

After a few minutes Lupe climbed back up the river bank carrying a short piece of rope. He turned to Hector and put a finger to his lips. Hector was puzzled but remained there and quiet. Then Lupe lay down at the top of the bank, at the grassy edge of the field, and Hector could no longer see him. By then Hector had accepted Lupe's ways, even though they often seemed strange, so he closed his eyes and waited, falling into a half-sleep.

Suddenly Lupe appeared out of nowhere, sliding down the gravelly bank. The rope was stretched tight and at the other end, not really resisting, but following in a careless sort of way, was a young *chivo*, a goat.

It was not full grown but still too much for two men to eat. Before Hector could even ask a question, Lupe gave the answer.

"A present, for Emilio," he said. "It is a fine goat, do you agree?"

"You will take the goat?" Hector asked. "It is still many kilometers, yes? And the way will be slower."

"A little slower, perhaps," he said, "but this I do every year. A gift for my oldest son."

"But it is not yours," Hector said. "The goat belongs to another man." But Hector was not bothered by that for he knew that a wolf or a coyote would have done as much.

"Many goats are in the field, but this one chooses to go with me. It is the same every year." Lupe looked back toward the field. "When I lie there," he said, "only one goat is wise enough to come near and not be afraid. Sometimes, in other years, none have come to me. If that happens I do not disturb them but move on to another field. Always there will be a field where one goat knows that it is mine. This year we are lucky, a fine goat and so easy."

The goat was eager to go and Hector found that it lightened his heart to see the goat prance at the end of the rope. When he needed to graze, they stopped, and the pace of the journey slowed by a little, but the way seemed easier.

As they moved north the land changed, the desert faded behind, and fields of corn stood high and withered on either side. Houses were hidden in groves of trees, soft in the distance, and during the day they could hardly escape the sound of a tractor. At night the lights of houses across the country blinked on and then off and the glow from small towns lit up the sky. They passed under a highway bridge and stepped around piles of cans and broken bottles while occasional cars hummed by over their heads.

Rubén's tortillas plus three dozen more from the market were gone. Along the way they had left a trail of orange rinds and now the small bag that held the fruit was empty. When Hector walked he felt his clothes slide over his bones and although he was still strong and could walk many more miles, he was hungry all of the time. Lupe had eaten very little, but with the food gone, Hector knew they must do something.

Lupe led the goat into the woods where the brush was thick and tied him to a small tree. The goat raised its head and made one high-pitched complaint as they left but then went to work on the lushness of new leaves.

At the bridge they climbed the bank, its clay slippery from a rain they had followed all morning, a rain that had trailed to the north and out of sight. At the top Lupe looked down the highway and pointed to a building near the road, only fifty meters to the west. A faded sign angled across its roof. Hector read it aloud. "The Riverside — Gas Gro Bait." A pickup truck rested under the overhang between the gas pumps and the door, and as they got nearer Hector saw a car at the side of the gray building, almost hidden by the shadows of the afternoon.

They stepped inside, Hector's hand deep in his pocket, gripping a thin fold of bills.

"Can I help you fellows?" a voice asked. The store was dark and cool. One man sat on a box that held cold drinks, and the other man, the one who spoke, leaned back in a chair behind a counter.

Lupe talked in his best English, making little bows in the same way he must have in his younger restaurant days, while Hector wandered to the back of the store. The meat counter was bright and had little meat but held a huge round of yellow cheese that glowed like a moon. In the whole store there was hardly any food not in a can or a package. Some Hector could read, some had pictures — coffee and fruit and beans and corn. The prices seemed very low, but then Hector remembered they were not marked in pesos but in the dollars of America. He felt overcome by the strangeness of everything and turned back to Lupe.

They had a tall orange drink and picked out a few things to carry. Lupe chose a package of cookies, chocolate layered with smooth cream, and four cans of tiny sausages and two of fish, then three cans of beans and a package of crackers. Hector squeezed a loaf of bread and picked it up, but it was limp and he put it back.

"It's yours." Hector looked around and the man behind the counter was now standing, gesturing at him.

"You handle the bread and you buy it," he said. He was angry at Hector for some reason and turned to the man who still sat on the drink box. "Goddamn Meskins," he said, "come in and handle everything in the store and buy five dollars worth of groceries."

Hector moved to Lupe's side. The man pointed to the bread and this time shouted at Hector. "Get it, it's yours. You've bought it."

Lupe went to the bread rack and picked a loaf off the top.

"Not that one. There." The man wagged his finger to the right. Lupe touched another loaf and the man nodded his head. "That's it." Then to the man, "Goddamn Meskins." The other man laughed and spit into a can on the floor.

Hector moved to the back again to see the cheese, but he was afraid to ask for any. He was not sure what would make the man angry. At the end of one aisle Hector stopped at a glass case that held a dozen knives, some large enough to butcher a calf, and others smaller, with handles of bone, their blades half way open. Hector tried to lift the lid, but it was locked. He motioned to Lupe. When he saw the knives he nodded his head and said, "Yes, they are fine knives."

Hector pointed to one with a single blade half as long as his hand. The man came quickly, carrying a ring of keys. Hector asked him how much, and the man answered and was no longer angry. Hector opened the knife, then closed it again. He balanced it in his hand and it felt right, like all well-made tools must.

They paid and left. When the screen door shut behind them the man said something Hector could not understand and the other man on the drink box laughed with a huge snort.

The beans from the can tasted strange, but Hector expected everything to be that way, and for what he had he was grateful. But it was hard to eat beans with no tortillas.

While they ate Lupe sailed the white slices of bread one at a time into the river and for a few minutes they watched the pieces dance and break on the river's surface as fish eagerly attacked them.

Lupe gave one cookie to the goat, and they started up the river once more, at first walking at the water's edge, but then, finding the ground too soft, moving to the top of the river's bank, skirting the edges of fields, staying in the trees as much as possible.

They came to the place where the small river joined with the Nueces and Lupe said that they should stop, even though the sun was still above the trees.

"Tomorrow, by this time we will be there," he said. The goat grazed on the young leaves of a tree, its front hooves balanced against the trunk.

"How will I get work?" Hector asked. "Where Emilio lives there is much work?"

"If not there then somewhere else," Lupe said. "You are young and strong so there will be no problem. For me it is different. No one will hire an old man. But sometimes I lay a stone pathway or repair a wall. A day or two is enough. Too much work I do not need."

That night Hector tried to sleep, but the mosquitoes were hungry and he listened to the trucks from a nearby highway until almost morning. But with the sun, his energy returned. That day, he thought, would be his last day of walking, maybe forever, for soon he would have a job and then a pickup, a dark blue one, and would drive everywhere he went.

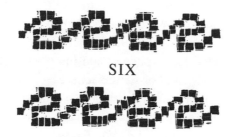

SIX

WHEN the river bent like the shoe of a horse they stopped. Lupe put his hand to his ear. They listened. In the distance a motor whined, then died, then whined again. "Chain saw," Lupe said, "brrr-rrr." He held his arms out and swung them slowly from left to right. Hector said "chain saw," then repeated the words over and over again. There were so many words to learn and so many sounded alike.

Soon they saw a man in a clearing of high grasses, a soft meadow that flattened out beyond the river. The man knelt in the shade of a pickup, the chain saw silent on the ground beside him. Beyond him the hills were covered with outcroppings of white stone and dotted with trees hardly higher than Hector's head. A place like this, Hector thought, perhaps this very ground, would be his home when he had worked and had much money. He gazed out at a piece of land that nestled against a white cliff. He would build his house solid on that shelf of rock, and Leticia would be there with the boys, and maybe another son or even a daughter. They would be waiting for him to return from his field, or perhaps he would have been in some nearby village, driving his own pickup, and he would return with fresh seed to be planted and his pockets filled with gifts for them all. For Leticia a necklace of bright stones from an American store and for Tomasito, a knife or a small bright flashlight so the darkness would never frighten him again. And for Efrán candy, hard and sweet, in wrappers that were smooth and bright.

When Hector came back from his dream Lupe was already halfway to the pickup, dragging the goat behind him, no longer moving like an old man. Hector hurried to catch up.

When the man saw Lupe with the goat he jumped to his feet with a great laugh. He called Lupe "Señor Lupe" and shook his hand with both of his for many minutes. Then Lupe introduced him to Hector. "This is Señor Herman, Emilio's *patrón*," and from the softness of his voice Hector knew that Señor Herman was a good man. He offered Hector his hand. It was rough and huge, his grip steady and true.

They rode in the pickup to Señor Herman's house, only a few hundred meters away, hidden in a thicket of squatty trees. Lupe and the other man talked while Hector listened, all the time keeping one eye on the goat who rode contentedly in the back.

The year had been bad it seemed. A late frost had killed the young fruit of the trees and the corn had not matured for lack of rain. Señor Herman could no longer afford to pay Emilio, and he had gone to Denver to be with his brother who had a good job. Without asking, Hector knew that there would be no work for him there. But Lupe asked for him anyway. Señor Herman just looked straight ahead and shook his head as if he were very tired.

Hector had forgotten so many things. To sit in a chair and eat from a table was part of being a man. He watched Señor Herman's wife — her name was Josie — as she brought bowls and platters of food to the table. She would make two of Leticia. All her talk was with questions: "What part of Mexico are you from?" Her voice was strong, full of sureness like a man's. "Comitan," Hector answered. "It is a small city. Far to the south." She nodded. Then, "Your first time in Texas?" and "Do you have a family?" and on and on until Hector was dizzy from finding the American answers in his head.

Hector watched how Lupe ate and did the same. They had bread made of corn that rose higher than twenty tortillas, but was too soft. The meat he didn't know. It was in a mound with the sweet red sauce of tomatoes on it. It, too, was soft. So this is the way they eat in America, Hector thought. Leticia would not like it, but in her own kitchen she could cook in the old ways. No one would have to know.

After the meal they moved to another room and the chair Hector took held him like the shawl of a forgotten mother. From the food and from the days of walking he felt heavy. Señor Herman talked to someone on the telephone; Hector's mind felt like that of an old man and he heard the words — work . . . Mexican . . . small . . . not much English — but became confused trying to understand.

Lupe listened to Señora Josie. He sat straight on the edge of a chair made of wood and watched her as if no other person had ever spoken to him before.

The room was warm. Hector's body floated on the softness of the chair. He had always been in that place and would be there forever. He would never move again.

"Stand up." Hector heard a voice that was strange. For a moment he was lost. "Hey, boy." The voice was louder, from across the room. Almost filling the frame of a door Hector saw a moon-faced man. "Stand up," he said again, "let's see how big you are." Hector looked at Lupe, who nodded his head and motioned Hector to rise. So he did.

Señor Herman explained that this man, who was called Tiemann, owned much land and many cows, a ranch he called it, not so many kilometers away.

Tiemann stared at Hector. Hector nodded and smiled. Tiemann shook his head. "They get scrawnier every year," he said. All the time he leaned against the

70

frame of the door and breathed heavily, as if the room had little air. "Have you worked with cows, with the *vacas*," he asked.

Hector looked at Lupe. His eyes were on the floor, but the old man nodded his head just a little. "Yes," Hector said, "for many years I have worked with the *vacas* in Mexico." A small smile crossed Lupe's face.

"You drive a tractor? You work with the *maquinas*?"

This time Lupe's head was still.

"A little," Hector said. "The tractor I drive a little."

"Humph," Tiemann snorted. "You can or you can't." He looked like a man who had eaten an apple too green. Hector knew he should not have lied.

Señor Herman said that maybe he could use Hector to work one day a week, and Hector thought, yes, that would be good. But Señora Josie made an angry sound and left the room.

Tiemann shook his head. "That never works," he said. "A man can't have two bosses. You found him," he said turning to Señor Herman, "you have first shot, but I don't share my boys with anyone." He looked at Hector again, his breathing still heavy, his eyes as dark as a river after a rain.

"You know the damn wetbacks," he said, "They'll play us against each other, and first thing you know they'll be making more than we do."

Tiemann looked around like he wanted to spit, then straightened up and took a step back, as if he were about to leave. He talked straight at Señor Herman, and Hector felt the bite of his words. "Yours or mine," he said. "I don't give a damn," and he looked at his watch. Señor Herman glanced toward the kitchen to see if his wife was there. Then he shrugged his shoulders. "I guess he's yours." The two men shook hands.

Hector moved over next to Lupe and asked, "What will you do? Where will you go?"

"To Denver, to Chicago," he said. "For me it is no great problem. A bus can take me to see my sons, all of them, wherever they are."

Then he leaned close to Hector all the while watching Tiemann and quietly spoke. "*Cuidado*, my friend, be very careful."

"Why? What do you mean?" Hector asked, but Lupe said no more.

"Let's go, boy," Tiemann said. Then he turned to Señor Herman. "What's he call himself?" he asked, a question that was Hector's to answer, and in his very best English he did.

"My name is Hector Rabinal," he said, and the words echoed around the room.

"Okay, Hector Rabinal," Tiemann said, "you and your things ride in the back of the pickup," and he jerked a thumb towards the door.

Outside in the yard, Lupe, with his little bow, said, "One moment, *por favor*." Then he turned to Hector. "My friend, you must have the goat, for in America it will not be possible for me to take. The buses, you see, they are very different here."

Hector looked at Tiemann, to see what he might say, if his new *patrón* would allow him to take the goat.

72

Tiemann didn't look at Hector, but shook his head and spoke to Señor Herman. "Goddamn Meskins and their goats," he said. Then he turned to Hector. "Okay, but keep the damned goat out of my hair. Understand?"

That puzzled Hector, but Lupe said, "He does not say no, so take him." So Hector did.

The back of the pickup was damp from the night air, but the air was cool, moving gently from the south. Hector drew deep breaths, knowing that by some miracle that same air might have been breathed by Leticia weeks before.

The pickup started. Hector closed his eyes and smelled the air, hoping to find something familiar. There was nothing but the odor of the goat who stood wide-legged next to him. That and the sourness of his own body.

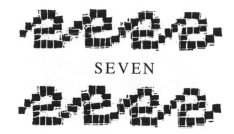

SEVEN

MY DEAREST LETICIA,
My sons for whom my fondness knows no end,

I am writing to you at last because finally I feel safe and
that I will be in one place a time long enough so that
you may answer, God willing. I trust that you are with
your brother Adolfo and his good family and that the
authorities will not pursue the innocent wife of a man
who has sinned against the state. Not against God, for a
man has no choice but to defend his home, and the
God of my father will, I am confident, forgive any act
committed to honor and protect my family. But for your
sorrow and suffering I beg forgiveness.

Today is a Sunday, sometime in the month of September. I know it is a Sunday not because I hear the bells of the *iglesia* calling me to mass, for the ranch (which is very grand and belongs to a man who is named Tiemann — yes, all the names in Texas are strange) is far from any church or any village, but I know it is Sunday because I have worked only one half of a day and the afternoon is my own..

My house is a trailer on wheels, though the wheels are rotten and have not rolled in many years. The trailer is small, but for only me is more than enough. It is not a house that you would know. The walls do not breathe, and the air inside is forever old. Most nights I choose to sleep outside on the hardness of the ground rather than bake in my oven house. But when the rains that fall race across its roof it is dry, and for that I am thankful. The water that I drink and with which I wash comes easily through a pipe not twenty paces away. Everything will be easy for you and every worry that you have will erase like chalk on Father Cota's schoolboard. Is there word about Father Cota? In Altomirano, in Mexico, where he now lives I visited him, and now my soul is cleansed. By his good graces (and that of my father's God) I am here in America. Be not afraid. Father Cota said there is no other way.

Tomasito, my son, your father will soon know how to drive a tractor, and perhaps a pickup. There are many things to learn, and I will teach you everything when you are with me again.

My *patrón* the first day brought two sacks for me: one

filled with dried *frijoles* the color of the earth that is near Chajul, not black like our *frijoles negros*, and the other with flour that slips white and smooth through my fingers. I have asked for corn that is ground, but my *patrón* is a very busy and important man and forgets many things. But, and this is important, I will soon be very rich, for everyone in this place has many things, and with my money I will send for you, my beloved wife and my treasured sons. Do not have sadness, for we will be together again *soon*.

With warm embraces,
Hector Rabinal

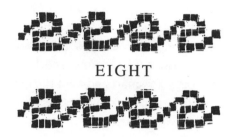

EIGHT

AFTER HE HAD EATEN his meal of tortillas and beans Hector fed Chivito — that is what he named his little goat — by wandering slowly from place to place in the dark, letting him graze. The rope was not too long, and although each day Hector staked Chivito in a new place, the ground all around the trailer that was his new home had been nibbled bare.

While Chivito grazed, Hector talked to him in the language of his father and the goat understood. Hector told him of his *finca*, how the ground was rich from the volcanic ash, how he dropped beans in a dark furrow and by the time he reached the end of the row he looked back to see the first seeds sprouting. Chivito believed everything Hector said.

He told the goat how Leticia, when she was young, allowed Hector to watch as she bathed in the stream, at first pretending she didn't know he was there in the trees, and later how she would take him to the stream with her and how the light from the moon swam across her skin, and the way her wet hair tasted in his hungry mouth. Tomasito was conceived in a quiet pool of that very stream. Water is a gift, and it gives back life in many ways. Chivito ate and listened. He understood. He was very smart and kept the rattlesnakes away.

While it was light Hector could not see Tiemann's house for the trees, but at night the lights glittered through the leaves. When at first he saw the house blazing at night Hector could not help but see the fire that consumed his own home. For weeks he relived that fire, but no more. Some nights he stood in the shadows outside the house of his *patrón* and watched as Tiemann drank his beer and stared at the flashing stories of the television. Most nights Hector watched until the house became dark, then lay next to Chivito and followed the tiny red lights that whirled across the sky.

Each morning Tiemann drove up in his pickup just at light. He took Hector down into a canyon where cedar trees grew thick. Since Hector had no tools with which to work Tiemann rented him an axe with two blades and a file to keep it sharp. All day he cut posts for fences. The posts had to be straight and the length of three axe handles. Hector had to cut twenty each day or he would not be paid. Tiemann said that was the way of work in Texas and that it was fair. Only two days had Hector fallen short of that number and that was when the axe was new to his hands.

Before dark Tiemann would come again and together they loaded the posts in his truck. The resin from the posts stuck to Hector's arms, and the dry cedar showered his back like dry rain. It stung through his sweat soaked shirt and matted in his hair.

On Saturdays at the end of the day it was different. After the posts were loaded and they started back out of the canyon Tiemann would hand Hector a beer that was cold. He would sip it slowly, finishing it each time with regret long after Tiemann had dropped him off at the trailer, savoring its last warm bitterness while he followed Chivito around the dark field.

Those nights, from Tiemann's house he would hear Saturday sounds, many voices, loud with laughter, and smell meat cooking over an open fire. And on those nights Hector was lonely enough to cry out in the night. Yes, that lonely. But he didn't and was thankful that the weariness of his body forced his mind into sleep.

One day the pickup did not take Hector into the canyon but through the village called White Hills and to another large farm. There a field was lined with bale after bale of hay. Men worked a machine which gobbled up rows of grass and then dropped the bales behind, tight and green. Tiemann drove the truck through the field while Hector swung the heavy bales on behind.

When the bales were stacked six high in the truck, Tiemann stopped to talk to the *patrón* of the farm and Hector waited in the shade of the hay. The two men laughed and argued all at one time as if they were both friends and enemies. One of the helpers, whose name was Roberto, came to Hector while he waited. He asked, "How long you have worked for Tiemann?" as if he knew Hector's *patrón* very well.

Almost six weeks, Hector told him.

"How much pay?" Roberto asked, and told Hector that he made fifteen dollars a day. Also that he lived in a grand trailer with only his brother, and his *patrón* gave them chickens and eggs and they had a small garden plot for chiles and tomatoes.

"How much pay for you?" he asked again, and Hector felt like a boy whose father was about to scold him for being foolish. For Hector had never asked. He was thankful for the work and the safety and the food. What did he need money for then? And what had been his choices? Tiemann would pay when Hector asked or when he left. He was very wealthy. That was no problem, but Hector did not say those things to Roberto, for he knew that he would not understand and would perhaps laugh at him, thinking him to be foolish.

So Hector simply said, "About the same. Yes, the same, *mas o menos*. My *patrón* is very fair. He is a man of honor."

Roberto laughed. "I have known many like you who work for Señor Tiemann. Never before has anyone called him an *hombre justo*. Six weeks," Roberto said. "Six weeks is much time to work as an *esclavo*."

"A slave?" Hector asked. "I am a slave for no one. What do you mean?"

Before Roberto could answer, Tiemann's voice boomed out over the field. "Hector! *Vámonos!* Let's get going." Tiemann turned to his friend. "Damned wet-backs'll talk all day if you let 'em."

Hector looked back at Roberto as they drove off. *"Cuidado,"* he softly said, "Be careful my friend."

On the way back Hector wanted to ask about his pay, but Tiemann was complaining about the cost of hay, how his friend who had the meadow was not a true friend at all, and how this year his calves were all born light and stunted because of the drought. Hector had the intelligence to know that was a time to listen and not to ask, so he listened and nodded and did not talk. Hector understood that Tiemann was only a man, more or less like himself, only his problems were different.

They stopped at a store in the village. "Super S," the sign above it read. Tiemann motioned for Hector to stay in the truck and he did, for he knew that he was illegal and no one could know where the border patrol might be.

The store had many customers. Hector watched them come and go. Some appeared to be Mexican, and Hector thought that perhaps they could be his friends at some later time, when his family had come to Texas. Perhaps he could get papers. It could be done, for Lupe had told him much about it.

A woman carrying two sacks of groceries left the store looking over her shoulder, first one way and then the other at her two children, scolding them to stay with her and watch for cars. She was about the age of Leticia but was taller and walked in a different way, stronger and surer, it seemed. Hector wanted to help her with the sacks or with her children. She was pretty. Perhaps, he thought, her husband was in Denver or Chicago, and she was lonely. Her breasts pushed against the sacks and her skirt was tight across her thighs. Hector felt his groin swell. He wanted Leticia, but right then he wanted that strange woman to be with him more than anything else. At that moment he cared about nothing else, not the border patrol or Tiemann or ever going home again. He wanted to be alone with that one strange woman.

Tiemann pushed his way out the door carrying a sack and walked by the woman as if she weren't there. He handed a can of orange drink through the window to Hector. Hector murmured thank you and felt a sense of relief, one of having been rescued, possibly from his own weak self. He laid his arm across his lap and felt the throb of his hardness, and he was both ashamed and angry. And for being angry he didn't know quite why.

That afternoon Hector hoed weeds from Señora Tiemann's garden of flowers. She was very proud and very particular and thought that Hector might not know the difference between a weed and a flower. Hector listened patiently to what she said, following her around the edge of the garden. She was a large woman with rough red hands and feet that were so swollen she wore slippers everywhere. Her hair she twisted around pink cylinders and she never smiled, as if to smile would break the hardness of her face. But later she did bring Hector a jar of water and ice. Hector knew that to drink cold water when you were hot weakens the body, but he drank it gladly.

Hector asked if perhaps there could be a letter for him, for it had been a few weeks since he wrote Leticia. The Señora looked at him and her face changed just a little, as if she had some small sadness within her. But she said no, there was no letter for him and turned away.

The gardens were clean of weeds before dark. Hector had raked the earth all in one direction and swept the rock walk that led to the barn. He was glad for one day not to cut the cedar posts. Tiemann stopped by and with a grunt told him to take the pile of weeds out behind the barn and then he could go. "Didn't get your twenty posts today," he said with a laugh, and Hector laughed, too, at his joke. Before Hector left, while Tiemann was in the barn, his wife brought him a sack. She glanced around for Tiemann and put a finger to her lips. "This is for you," she said. "You did a good job. Now go."

In the trailer Hector emptied the sack, one thing at a time. A jar of ground coffee, then fat links of sausages, a handful of slender red peppers and wrapped sticks of butter. For one night no one could eat better. If Roberto were there he would see. Hector Rabinal was living a good life.

That night Chivito pulled him around the field by

his rope. He was bigger now, almost grown, and no longer content to stay in one place. Hector's hands were lazy, his mind at ease. At that moment, that hour of that star-streaked Texas night, he had contentment for the first time in many months.

"Señor Tiemann," Hector asked the next morning, and even the way he began the question brought a cloud to Tiemann's face. They were bouncing along the rough road to the cedar canyon and although last night Hector had slept easily, he awoke with many thoughts. Tiemann looked quickly at Hector and then again straight ahead.

"Can you, *por favor*, tell me about my pay? I know you are a fair man, but I need to know the dollars that my pay will be. Many important things depend on it."

"You planning on leavin'?" Tiemann asked. "That's about what I figured. About the time I get you trained to do a day's work you leave. You boys can't seem to stay in one place long enough to do any good."

"No," Hector said, "you do not understand. I am content to remain here and work. Perhaps I can drive the tractor better and learn much more from you. But the pay I need to know."

"Well," Tiemann said, guiding the pickup to a stop, "the pay is fair, but not so simple. You give me a few days and I'll figure it up. Most times I wait until a boy is ready to leave to pay. It's safer that way. Too many temptations here in Texas for you Meskins, you know."

Hector stepped down from the truck with his axe and jug of water. But for a minute he didn't close the door.

"A few days will make no difference," he said. "I have much patience, but I am a man, and a man needs to know his pay."

"Okay, I hear you," Tiemann said and reached over to slam the door shut. "I said a few days. I'll let you know, but for now I'm tired of your damned whining. You're not happy here, no one's keeping you. You know a better deal, you can take off. I don't give a damn. Wets are swarming all over, anyway, like a bunch of goddamned fire ants."

That day Hector's axe moved on its own, and the cedar fell like stalks of dry corn. When Tiemann came for him the posts were too many to stack in the back of the truck.

"About time you put in a day's work," Tiemann grunted, but Hector could tell he was surprised at the number of posts.

On Sunday Hector cut posts until the sun was high and stopped a few minutes to rest and eat his beans wrapped in tortillas. Sunday afternoons he was free to wash his clothes or sleep or soak beans and make tortillas for the next week. He waited in the shade of a limestone ledge for Tiemann to rattle down the canyon road and soon fell asleep. Later, when he wakened to the fuss of a blue jay, Tiemann still had not come. It was Sunday. Hector was sure. He marked each day as it passed. So he left the pile of posts and walked out of the creek bottom. The weather had started to cool, and he did not mind. It was no farther than he walked each day in Huitupan.

From his trailer Hector could hear laughter and loud talk at Tiemann's. Tiemann and his friends had many fiestas, and Hector longed to be with his friends and with his family, sitting by a stream, watching his sons playing in the water. Leticia would be cooking a pot of *guisado*, and a jug of *posh* or even some beer from Chajul would be cooling in the stream.

He shook the cedar from his shirt and bent over to let the water from the faucet rush over his head. He filled a bucket for Chivito and carried it to the shade of an oak tree where he had tied the goat that morning. Chivito was no longer there.

He is a bad goat, Hector thought, always he wants to be where he isn't. The way I am. We both are not in our right places. That is why we are friends.

Hector whistled for Chivito, for the goat knew the sound he made and answered, even if he did not always come. All Hector could hear was the fiesta at Tiemann's house. He made a circle through the woods, watching for signs, calling out *"flojo,* lazy one, where are you?"

Tiemann was at the back of his house. He and two friends sat in metal chairs that rocked. They drank beer and laughed. Their words all ran together. Why do *Americanos* talk so fast, Hector wondered. Señora Tiemann came from the house with more beer. She was drinking one also, out of the bottle, as if she were a man.

Hector took off his hat as he approached them. He stopped at the edge of the flower garden and stood there a few minutes. He was quiet and they did not see him.

Finally, Señora Tiemann noticed him and touched her husband on the shoulder. Then she left. Tiemann said something to the other men. They drank their beers and watched. Hector did not like the way they looked. They wore caps as if they were not old, but still boys who played *beisbol*.

"Señor Tiemann," Hector said. He held his hat behind him. "My *chivo*, my goat — have you seen him?"

Tiemann frowned and shook his head. "You see a goat around here?" he asked Hector, who then looked around. "You boys see a goat walking around here anywhere?"

His friends laughed and shook their heads. One of them crushed his beer can in one hand, as if you must be strong to do so. But Hector knew better.

"Damned goats have a way of disappearing," Tiemann said. Then he stood up and moved to a metal box on wheels. He opened the lid and smoke swirled all around. He turned the charred meat on the grill and closed the lid.

"I told you to keep your damned goat away from my old lady's flowers," Tiemann said. "Just a damned nuisance is all he was."

Then one of Tiemann's friends said, "A goat is only waiting to be *cabrito*."

Señora Tiemann was to one side and Hector looked at her. She sipped her beer, then looked down at the grass, moving something with her toe. Everyone was quiet, waiting.

Then Tiemann said, "Okay, I'll pay you for the damned goat." He reached for his wallet and pulled out some bills.

"The *chivo* was mine," Hector said. "He was mine to feed, to care for, and he was mine to kill and to eat. I also know that a *chivo* is fine for eating. I have eaten it many times. And this goat, also, I would have killed and would have eaten and been thankful. But it was not for you to do, but for me."

"Hell, boy, it was just a goat," Tiemann said and reached in the cooler beside him. "Here, have a beer."

For a moment Hector thought not of the beer that Tiemann held, but of his machete. But only for a moment. He said no and turned away, walking until the trees hid him, and then he ran the rest of the way to the trailer.

It took but a few minutes for Hector to gather his things. His shirt was still damp, but he pulled it on. He wrapped tortillas around what beans were left and filled his jug with water.

When he reached the edge of the yard Tiemann was waiting. He pulled a roll of bills from his pocket. His friends talked quietly to each other and watched. Señora Tiemann was nowhere around.

"I figured you'd be taking off," Tiemann said. "The way you talked the other day I could tell. Take this," he said. "I figured it up last night." He handed Hector the money and said, "Even Steven," and one of the other men laughed.

"How much?" Hector asked.

Tiemann pulled out a paper he had written on and read it. His words were quick but Hector heard it all.

"Twelve dollars a day, less three a day for rent, three a day for groceries, fifty cents a day for the axe. The water, the lights, they're free. Four days you didn't make the quota. Total one hundred and sixty dollars."

Hector counted it out and tried to figure if it was right. How many *quetzals* would it be in Guatemala? How many *pesos* in Mexico? Could that be enough for Leticia to come to Texas? Maybe enough to start a house? Would Roberto laugh if he could see how little? Hector had no way to know. He only wanted to leave. But where would he go? He turned and walked away. Tiemann snorted like a horse. Hector heard the angry sound of beers popping open. He never looked back.

NINE

TO GO SOUTH was all he knew. Nearer to Mexico, a place where the rhythms and the sounds of the people would embrace him. Someone there would help him. Leticia would not have lived where her husband was not treated as a man. She would find a contented way of life nearer the border. It was still Texas, still the United States and there would be much money for Hector to earn. The dollars from Ticmann were deep in his boot and with each step pressed against his calf and reminded him why he was there.

The way back down the river was easy, but the days were strange, like days not on a calendar, but that had been added; days that would not count in the days of his life. Everything he passed was familiar — he had seen it all before — but this time he moved as a stranger to his body, almost gliding across the skin of the earth.

When he reached out he could slip his hand into the brittle hearts of trees. The goats in the fields were only circles of whitened bones and he could see through the blackness of the wings of buzzards as they circled.

At night his body sank into the ground and voices from below spoke to him in his father's tongue. When he awoke a circle of rocks surrounded him. Fire leaped from the twigs he gathered as he stacked them. The tortillas in his pack smelled of smoke, like that of his house as it burned. The grass he pulled for his nightly bed wept and by morning he awoke to the smell of Leticia's damp hair, but he was alone.

Hector found it much simpler to move to the south, the direction of his home, than it had been to pull away to the north. And to have American dollars was not a bad thing. There was so much to buy. Even in the smallest country store he would wander up and down the aisles, not quite believing the many choices. In one store he could find nothing that was outside of a package. Not a squash or a pepper or an egg. He bought small cakes that were sweet and dark with chocolate. Inside of each one, Hector found a puff of sweet cream. They cost very much, but he ate them every day.

After six days the river widened, the land flattened out, and he knew he was nearing Laredo. Along the hard-topped road the pickups were filled with

Mexicans, going and coming to the fields of onions and lettuce and cotton. Other plants he did not know. Everyone had a pickup truck or a car. Even the women drove them. The music from their radios rushed by him, louder than the engines of the cars.

Hector Rabinal was the only man in Texas who walked.

At a station for gas where the stream of pickups stopped he asked for work. The man told him to talk to the other Mexicans who stopped by. He did, but it was not easy. The men, he could tell, were afraid of strangers, fearing that Hector might take a job from them or their brothers or cousins.

So Hector squatted in the shade of the building and waited. He studied the faces of the drivers who passed. He tried to imagine where they came from and if they left their mothers or brothers behind and how many days it took for them to find work and how long before they owned the shiny pickups.

It was late but not yet dark when a woman drove up. Her pickup seemed to float softly and was the color of a rose. Never had Hector seen a pickup that color, as smooth and pink as the lips of a beautiful woman. The woman moved toward the store, and Hector silently watched. She wore overalls over a pink shirt and a pink bandana bound her hair back in a long tail. Her skin was pale and glowed in the last sun of the day. She was not young, her hair had streaks of gray and her skin had seen many years of sun, but she moved quickly, as if she were still a señorita.

If her husband had been there Hector would have asked for work. Perhaps she had a garden brown with sagging tomato vines or potatoes still to be dug, or corn with hard and shiny kernels ready to be shucked and shelled for the winter, and beans, perhaps, dry and cracking on their brittle vines. Or young plants that would flourish in the cool fall nights; cabbages for soup, winter squash, even cilantro that would not bolt.

Or perhaps her husband was rich and had a tractor, an orange or a red one, that Hector could drive to break the earth of his enormous field. Or he could shear the man's sheep, watch over his goats. The woman would mail his letters to Leticia and perhaps teach him better English so never again would there be mysterious packages in the store or puzzling signs by the road.

The woman came out carrying a sack that was full. The man of the store was with her. He gestured to Hector. Come, his hand said, and Hector scrambled to his feet.

The woman asked his name and he told her. She extended her hand as if she were a man. She took Hector's and after one firm shake released it. Her name was Bonnie, a strange name, for some little known saint, perhaps. Hector did not know.

Señora Bonnie spoke the language of a Mexican with the man of the store, very rapidly. As she spoke she moved one hand like the flutter of a small bird's wings. Three bracelets of silver looped around her wrist and slid up and down as she talked.

"So you want work," she said. Her eyes gathered

Hector into her mind. "Where are you from? Where are you going? What do you know how to do?" Her questions jumped out at Hector all at once.

"I have worked in the north," Hector said, "on a very fine ranch many kilometers from here. This place here, Laredo, will be my home if I find work that is good, for someone who is fair."

"And where do you come from?" she asked again, as if it mattered to her, and she pointed to the south, across the river.

And for that concern Hector was grateful, for where he was from mattered to him. "My family — my wife, my two sons — they live far to the south." As Hector spoke he waved his arm in the direction of Mexico, beyond Mexico. But she couldn't have known that. Hector had not lied. He would not have wanted her to be dishonest with him. There had been more than enough dishonesty.

She asked if Hector could garden, if he could operate the machine that cuts the grass, if he could paint a house.

Hector answered yes to everything.

Señora Bonnie nodded and said *adiós* to the keeper of the store. Hector put his bundle in the back of her color-of-a-rose pickup and started to climb over the tail gate. But Señora Bonnie said, "No, up here." She looked back at the pack. "That is all?" she asked.

"All," Hector said.

"Then *vámonos,*" she said. "Let's go."

While Señora Bonnie carried the sack of groceries

into her house Hector waited out front in the yard. He was full of questions and uncertainty. Should he have asked to carry the sack for her? It was not too heavy. But should he have? Tiemann had told him to never come into his house. But she was not Tiemann. So much to learn.

He would watch. He would learn quickly.

Where were her husband or her mother or her sisters or her children? No woman could live alone, he thought. But just the day before he would have said that no woman would drive a color-of-rose pickup and wear a man's overalls. So who could know?

Señora Bonnie's house was grand. The roof of tiles glowed red from the *barro* of the earth. The walls were made of mud and straw and stood solid. Their cracks did not run deep. The house had four or perhaps five rooms, enough for two or more families. The windows were small, but all of glass. The door in front was solid and painted the blue of precious stones. The ground was covered with grass, short and fine as the hair of a cat, the kind Señora Tiemann had. The kind of grass, when it was cut, Chivito could smell from Hector's trailer. Perhaps he could have another Chivito here. The machine for cutting grass would not be necessary then. He would see.

Señora Bonnie stepped out from behind the house and waved for Hector. In the back plants and gardens were everywhere. The sun was gone, the air was still and cool, and tiny moths fluttered from blossom to blossom, unsettled in the harsh light from the back porch.

Señora Bonnie waited at the door of a small house that stood thirty paces behind her own, holding the screen door open. "This will have to do," she said, as if apologizing for providing Hector a place to sleep.

It was dark when Hector stepped inside, but she touched a switch and a single ceiling bulb lit up the room. A bed that stood on four long legs was in one corner. Hector touched it and felt it thick with feathers. A stove and sink and a tank for hot water stood lined against one wall. A refrigerator hummed in another corner. The floor was smooth and hard and clean. The ceiling was white and seamless. Three walls had glass windows. Señora Bonnie raised one of them. It slid easily, and she propped it with a smooth stick. She opened the only other door and Hector could see that it was a *baño*. A fine house. Large enough for Hector's entire family.

Then Bonnie turned to face him. Hector could tell that something was written across her shirt, but the words disappeared into her overalls. He wondered what the shirt of a woman such as that would say.

"Okay, Hector," she said, and he could tell that what came next would be important. "This is the way it is." Her eyes were bright and as blue as the paint of her front door. She tossed her head as she talked and her hair waved from side to side sweeping across her neck. "If you work out, seventeen and a half dollars a day. And you get this." She waved her hand around the room and the bracelets jingled. "Six days a week. Off on Sundays. You pay for your own food. One six-pack a week. Beer, I'm talking about. You understand. Six *cervezas* a week. No more. No *amigos* over, no parties. No *amigas*, either. *Comprende?* You understand?"

"It is very clear," Hector said. "But when will I be paid, *por favor?* Another *patrón*, the one to the north, he was not fair." And Hector started to explain, but she stopped him.

"Saturdays," she said. "Cash, U. S. of A. dollars every Saturday. Okay?"

Hector said yes, that would be good. Again she shook Hector's hand. It was as if they had just traded two sheep for one goat.

"Early," she said. "Tomorrow, the sun is up, you are up, too. Understand?"

Hector nodded.

"You need food tonight?" she asked.

Hector had two of the round cakes of chocolate. They were perhaps pressed flat and melted, but they would do. "Tomorrow, yes, I will need more to eat. But for tonight there is no need. *Gracias.*"

Señora Bonnie nodded and moved out the door and into her garden. She stopped here and there to pull dried heads from the flowers. Then she disappeared into her house and the back porch light went out.

It was dark out. The night was quiet. Hector pulled his boots off. They would have to be re-soled soon. Too many kilometers. He filled a glass with water, cold from the tap. He settled into the grand chair. It was soft. He sank deeply in. The cakes of chocolate were mashed, but the rich cream had not escaped. A moth circled the light above as if it were a glowing moon and the bulb was its sun.

When Hector awakened the morning outside his window was gray and fast becoming lighter. The bulb above him still gleamed and three moths slept on the ceiling around it. He could hear the sounds of pickups and buses, but all bound together, for the house was away from town and hidden from the road by scrubby trees. Everyone was going to work early, and Hector was thankful to be joining them.

He pulled back the blanket from the bed and lay down, but for only a minute. If the bed were firmer, more like a mat on the floor it would be better, but it was what Señora Bonnie thought was right for Hector, so he would use it. He left the blanket pulled back, as if the bed had been slept in all night.

He ran water into the basin and washed his face, then with the bar of soap scrubbed the stain that ringed his hat and rinsed it carefully. It would never be new again, but the straw gleamed in the light above the sink. He made coffee that was thick and dark. He longed for sugar and milk and *pan dulce*. But many things he longed for he could not have, so for the moment he made himself content and did not mind.

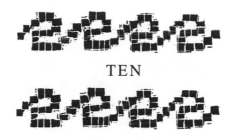

TEN

NEXT to the grand house, already in place, were a ladder and a saw and a pair of leather gloves. Señora Bonnie sipped coffee as she talked. Hector would paint her house but first all the branches from the trees and bushes had to be trimmed away. She still wore the overalls but that morning had on a different shirt, one that said something else that Hector could not quite see, and on her feet, sandals made of rubber. Her toenails glistened red in the early light.

While Hector cut the limbs she piled them into a wheelbarrow and carted them out back. He worked fast, the cutting was easy for him and the ladder moved down the wall like a giant insect. The stack of limbs rose with the sun.

At noon Señora Bonnie brought Hector a plate of chicken and rice. She said that after work that day they would go to town for his food. "I will advance you money," she said, "if you need it."

Hector shook his head. "No," he said. "This is Wednesday, is it not? And you said you would pay on Saturday. That is our agreement. Already I have enough money for food." Hector was not as sure as he sounded, but she smiled as if she liked what he said. He would count his dollars carefully and buy little.

On the way to town Hector was not sure, but it did not seem right to be riding while a woman drove. Leticia would never drive a pickup, of that he was certain. But Hector did not know if he would have been able to have keep the truck in the road, especially at the speed Señora Bonnie drove. So fast, although town was but a few kilometers away. It was if they must hurry, but for what reason Hector did not know. The work for the day was completed. The night would be too long to be filled only with sleep. Perhaps Señora Bonnie was a person who was always in a hurry, even when there was nothing special to do.

Long green squash and onions and garlic and beans and cilantro, *manteca* and ground corn for tortillas, salt and rice and more coffee and a chicken bound tight in plastic with no feet, no head — all went into Hector's cart. Then a heavy sack of sugar and a cold block of white cheese. He tried to count the dollars it all would cost, but the basket filled too fast.

Señora Bonnie found for him bars of soap and tooth-paste and a small brush. Hector chose green chiles and tomatoes, a liter of orange drink and the chocolate cakes. And one six pack of beer. "For one week," she told him again.

Her basket filled, also, but was different. Two bottles of wine, one red and the other clear, lettuce and toma-toes, plastic sacks of brittle pastas, and other packages Hector did not know that were frozen hard with color-ful pictures of food. All very fine and expensive.

The store gleamed with many lights and music float-ed from the ceiling while they shopped. The women all wore clothes bought from the store and their children wore shoes and held brightly colored boxes of candy and small trucks and balloons.

Hector wanted his sons to learn how it was in Texas. They too would go to that store with their mother and run up and down the aisles, choosing whatever they might want. Hector would wait outside in his pickup and talk with the other men about *futbol* and the num-ber of pigs that his sow had birthed and the ways to pol-ish a truck so that it gleamed. His radio would play whatever music he wanted, loud enough so that his friends might share his good fortune. They would plan a small fiesta for Sunday where there would be as much *cerveza* as they wanted and they would eat *cabrito* if they desired, and if not eat many packages of hot dogs the way Americans did.

And the women would watch the children and talk of their sisters and their babies and when it became dark they would brush their straight black hair until it sparkled with flashes of fire, and whisper among themselves, and later take their men to their houses, to the quiet of their rooms, and let them know their soft secrets and welcome their hardness with small cries in the dark and afterwards light many candles and talk softly of dreams. Dreams of what was and what would be.

For a week he trimmed the limbs from the house, and then with a stiff broom and soapy water washed away the old loose paint and dirt. Señora Bonnie came back from town, the pickup heavy with gallons of paint and sacks of cloths and brushes and rollers. The paint was the same color as her pickup and rolled on smoothly. The skin of the house drank the paint thirstily, and Hector emptied many buckets each day.

The half that was completed shone like a wildflower in a barren field. Señora Bonnie was pleased. She stood beside Hector, then motioned for him to follow. "I need a little help," she said. They walked around the house. The morning air was cool, the wind fresh out of the north. A scattering of leaves blew across the newly withered grass. To the side of the yard stood a row of fruit trees, a few yellow leaves still clinging to their branches. Here and there an apple or a peach, shrunken and dried, hung from a bare branch.

Señora Bonnie took a small limb from one of the apple trees and gave it a pull, then twisted it from side to side. "No," she said, "not enough give." Then she took another, and then still another. "Okay," she finally said and handed Hector a small pair of cutters from her pocket. She pulled the branch down and held it steady with both hands. "Now, Hector," she said, "cut it here, above this joint," and Hector slid the clippers slowly up the branch until she nodded. "That's good," she said, and Hector cut. The limb was long, but with the cutters she made two quick cuts, trimming the branch until it had the shape of a Y and was hardly longer than her hand.

"I need two more," she said, and they moved to a peach tree. She found the right limb. Hector cut, she trimmed. This they did once more until she had three.

"A workday for me," she said. "Gotta find some folks a little water."

Hector was puzzled.

"You know?" she asked. "In Mexico, too, there are *brujas*, aren't there? That's what I am, a *bruja* who finds water. A water witch."

"Yes," Hector said. "I understand. You will use the green limbs of the trees to find water. No?"

"You got it," she said. "A strange way to make a dollar, huh?"

"For me? No, it is not strange at all. To find water without the green limbs of fruit trees, to see through the earth to the pools of water, that would be strange. In my country one shaman in our village could find water in the same way. To find water is a gift. It is sacred. But a shaman who finds the water, who blesses with the

107

water, who cleanses with the water, is not a *bruja*, not a witch. In my country a *bruja* is something different."

Señora Bonnie laughed. "Well, for some people in this country a witch is something different, too. I had a husband once who called me a witch, and for sure it had nothing to do with finding water. And nothing at all to do with being cleansed or blessed. Oh no, you can be sure of that."

Hector thought he understood. She has had a husband but does no more, for he thought she was a witch. That had happened in Huitupan, also. But Señora Bonnie looked like no witch he had ever seen. Her skin was light. Waves of golden hairs ran across her arms. She sparkled when she talked and bounced when she moved. She had the body and the face of a younger woman, but Hector could tell by her hair and by the wrinkles at her eyes, by the skin on the backs of her hands that she had more years than he.

When she drove off Hector began to paint the house once more. He tried to remember in some detail the past few months, but everything in his mind seemed to be fading away or mixing together. Rafael and his bone-thin daughter from Peregrina were only names. Lupe was no longer an old man but the ghost-like memory of a laugh and a toothless grin; Tiemann no longer was red-faced and huge but as washed-out as a blue bowl of milk. Even Father Cota had weakened in his mind.

No longer could he close his eyes and see Leticia's face, only her last cry as she called his name stayed with him; even his sons had moved into all the other bodies of children he had seen until he could no longer separate them.

While he painted the house the color of a rose, Hector could see only the face of Señora Bonnie. He knew that that was wrong, that he was being foolish like a boy. It was not right for him to be a man and have such feelings. But he could not help it.

As he painted he looked into the house. The small window was for the bathroom. Its walls were covered with tiles and thick towels, and shelves held many-colored bottles that he did not know.

He worked down the wall, squeezing behind the bushes he had trimmed. In the next room he saw a bed covered with a white satin bedspread. On the walls glittered *milagros* of all kinds, made of tin and alpaca and silver and brass, hearts and heads and animals and limbs, but mostly hearts. One large *milagro* heart over the bed was surrounded by dozens of smaller hearts.

A table along one wall was filled with candles, tall ones in silver holders, small votive candles and bunches of thin, brightly colored candles stuck to the table by their melted wax, and those in painted glasses that bring good fortune and those with the *Virgen de Guadalupe* painted on them. It was as if the room were a church and the table an altar.

Paper flowers were everywhere, single flowers and bunches, yellows and red and different shades of blue. On one wall hung robes of many colors; ceremonial robes with arrows and darts of lightning and flashes of sun. Some Hector thought he had seen before on fiesta days at Chajul; most he had never seen, but he felt their strength and their power. Señora Bonnie had been to Chajul? Could she know his country? Perhaps she was a *bruja* or a even a shaman of some mysterious sort. He must be careful, he thought, of what he said, even of what he thought, for she might read into his heart or know his thoughts before he had thought them.

He painted around each window carefully and covered the wall with many layers of paint, as if that room of Señora Bonnie's were a sacred place.

He stopped when it became too dark to see where he had painted. By then his arms and his hands were the color of a rose and seemed to glow in the half-dark of the evening. As he washed the color from his arms it pooled like blood on the brown earth below him and splattered across the tops of his boots.

By the light that filled the room Hector wrote two letters. First, to Leticia in care of her brother at Todos Santos, giving her his new address and telling her that he was well and that this would be a fine place for them to live. He didn't tell her everything, not about the refrigerator and the stove with four flames and the bed that was filled with feathers. He didn't tell her that his *patrón* was a woman who drove a pickup. Leticia would understand better if she were here.

He wrote to Father Cota, also, telling him of both his good and bad fortune, for he knew Father Cota would understand how both together made a life complete. For it to be otherwise would be something different than any man could know. He asked Father Cota to contact

Leticia if he could, to let her know where he was in case she didn't get his letter, and to tell her to write to him there, so that he might know what he should do — when he could best send for them and how they could safely receive his dollars and slip out of Guatemala.

Afterwards in the dark he lay on his bed and listened to the sounds of the night — the coyotes as they chased a rabbit or cat through the brush, the sound of trucks and buses as they slowed with their blat-blat-blat, complaining as they eased into the edge of town.

Later, out of all the other noises of the night, he picked out the hum of Señora Bonnie's pickup well before its lights swam across the shadows of his room. He lay on his back and his body tensed. In his mind he saw the rose-colored door of her truck as it opened and she swung lightly out onto the ground. In her hand she held the three sticks that can find water, those that they cut in the afternoon. They would be too dry to use again and as she moved to the house she tossed them onto a pile of leaves that Hector would gather and burn the next day.

There was one silent moment before the back door opened, before the lights of the house went on. She hesitated. In the dark she would try to see the wall he had painted, the way the new color had changed her house, but it was too dark. She turned then, perhaps, and looked toward Hector's small room. He was silent in the dark and for a minute did not breathe.

Then the door to her house opened and quickly closed with a swish and a bang and the lights from one room and then another illuminated the backyard. For awhile sounds came from the kitchen — water running, a dish in the sink, bottles rattling as the refrigerator opened and closed. Then all but one light went out and music like Hector had never heard moved softly through the air. In a few minutes he heard the sound of water from the bathroom shower as it sprayed for a long time. Then silence, and Hector knew she was drying her body with one of the thick towels, and he could lie there and see it all. Her skin was pale in the bright light, her hair was darker when wet, but still the color of fine beer. The hairs under her arms were the same, but between her legs the fleece was lighter and spun from golden threads.

He found his hardness in the dark and moved and moved and moved until his breath came sharp and shallow and wetness filled his hand.

But it was not enough, it was never enough, and Hector fell asleep still restless and empty.

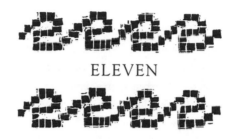

ELEVEN

BY MID-MORNING Hector had finished painting the house. He stood back to inspect his work and slowly walked the length of the back wall, touching a spot he had missed or brushing a place where the paint was thin. When Señora Bonnie brought a glass of water with ice to Hector, she surveyed the wall from end to end and then nodded. "A nice job," she said. "Very well done." Hector drank the water slowly to hide his smile.

"You have painted before?" she asked. "In Mexico?"

"Yes, Señora Bonnie, a little," he said.

"Not Señora Bonnie," she said. "Just Bonnie."

Hector looked at her to make certain and she said, "Yes, I insist."

"You are the *jefe.*" Hector said with a shrug, and they both laughed.

Bonnie started to move pots of flowers from under a tree out to where there was more light, where the winter sun threw its curve of brightness upon the ground.

Without asking, Hector could tell that she wanted him to help. He could tell, also, that she wanted to talk, that even a woman in her own country could be lonely and feel, perhaps, the way he did.

"Where else have you been in the United States?" she asked as they worked. "Do you know America?"

Hector thought that no, he did not know much of America, but he answered, "Yes, I know it very well," and began to say the names of places that he had heard. "Texas," he said first, and Bonnie laughed and said that didn't count.

"California," Hector then said. "And New York." He hesitated, trying to remember the places that Father Cota had taught him, the cities he had heard Lupe talk about, the places where the old man's sons lived. "Ah, Chicago," Hector said, "and Denver, and Canada, all to the north."

As he said that he looked to the north, away from the Rio Grande that was close enough to smell when the wind blew warm from the south.

"That's good," Bonnie said. "You do know many places." She stopped for a moment. The pots of flowers were where the sun would touch them until it was night.

"And to the south?" she asked. "You must know many places to the south."

Hector turned to face that direction, the way from which he had first come. "And there," he said with a wave of his hand, "is Mexico. And Nicaragua."

"And Guatemala?" Bonnie asked. Hector's heart felt both light and heavy at once, filled with both an elusive hope and an always present dread, but he would not let her know. "Yes, Guatemala." But his mind had gone as bare as a winter field, and he could name no more. Bonnie helped him.

Panama, she said, and he said Panama. And Brazil, she said, and he said Brazil, and the countries slipped in and out of his mind. Chile, Bonnie said, and he said Chile. Colombia, and he said, yes, Colombia. Argentina. Yes, Argentina. Venezuela. Yes, Venezuela.

Hector felt dizzy. "So many places to the south," he said. "So many to the north." And he felt that all at once the world was much larger than he had ever known, that it was revolving around him, at that place, on that tiny square of land where he stood. "It is true," he said, "that where we are, next to your house, must be the very center of the world."

Bonnie got a strange look on her face for a moment and cocked her head to one side. Then a smile crept slowly across her face, and she nodded her head three or four times. "Well, Hector," she finally said, "I'd never thought of it quite that way, but yes, I suppose it's true.

Wherever we happen to be, and we do both happen to be right here, right now, may well be the center of the world."

And with that she reached out and grasped Hector's arm right above the wrist and gave it a soft squeeze, just longer than for a moment. "Hector Rabinal," she said, "you're not an ordinary man. You know that, don't you?"

And what she said was something that Hector had always known, but had never heard.

"But is that a good thing," he asked, "to be not ordinary?"

"A very good thing," Bonnie said, "if you know what to do with it." She backed away then and gazed around the yard. "And what you need to do with it now is help me build a stone walk. So *vámonos*, let's go."

She grabbed some gloves from the back porch, and they took off in her pickup, the wind whipping her hair so that fine strands stuck in the corner of her mouth as she talked. She said she wanted to lay a stone walk from her back door, one that would lead out into her garden and wind around the plants and end up at Hector's small place.

To do that they needed flat rocks, so Bonnie drove north a few miles to what from above appeared to be a dry stream bed at the bottom of a deep gorge. Bonnie stopped the pickup at the edge. She slid out and motioned for Hector to follow. Cliffs of limestone dropped off many meters.

"Devil's River Canyon," she said and stared down into it as if she wanted to say more, but she didn't.

Hector could see no way to drive a pickup to the bottom, but Bonnie found a ragged, winding trail that they bumped down for many minutes. Finally they stopped on a bed of chalky gravel that felt solid. It was terraced with layers of leaves and brush left by early fall rains. Bonnie found a rock that was wide and flat, and said, "This is what we want."

Hector asked how many, and she laughed and patted the fender of the truck as if it were a burro. "As many as she'll carry," she said, and they started loading.

As Hector gathered rocks, hauling two or three at a time and shoving them scraping across the pickup bed, he noticed the small, clear trickle of water. We would not call this a river in my country, he thought, but then he looked up and saw the sheer walls that had been cut by centuries of wind and rushing water, and the almost black-blue of the sky, as if he were looking from the bottom of a dug well, and knew that, yes, this was indeed a river.

There were footprints in the wet sand near the shallow stream of water and as Hector sweated and sorted and lifted and carried he thought about those footprints and whose they might have been. They all were headed upstream away from the border. They were mostly made by boots, the heels digging unevenly into the sand, as if they were worn or their owner had staggered from fatigue. They could have been the footprints of someone that Hector had known or someone he had seen. Perhaps someone as ignorant as Hector had been who would turn up hungry at a place like

Tiemann's with hopes that would slide away like that loose sand.

But by chance or good fortune Hector was there working for a *patrón* who paid him and treated him as more than some oxen in a field. The sun was hot, the sky was clear, and the rocks seemed to weigh no more than smooth bundles of cloth.

They made two trips in the morning and another two in the afternoon, and the stack of rocks grew like a small mountain. It was strange, not to work with a woman, for Hector had done that many times before, but never had he worked beside a woman who did the work of a man. A woman who was strong and knew the ways a man worked, using the angle of her body to lift, positioning herself above each rock so that she would stay strong for a lifetime of rocks, if it should be necessary, pacing herself so that at the end of the day there would be strength enough left to be more than an animal that lay down at night only to dread the next day, for that would be a life not fit for anyone.

As they reached the top of the cliff with the last load, the canyon was all hidden in shadow. They stopped there where the country stretched out all around, empty of trees, just rolling sand and jagged outcroppings of rock.

"Come here," Bonnie said. "Let me show you something." She led him to the edge again and pointed to a place downstream from where they had taken the rocks. "What do you see?" she asked.

At first Hector could see nothing, for the canyon was

as blue as deep water, but then his eyes opened to the darkness and he made out a shape, that of a heart, cut out of a bank of gravel. Across the heart at an angle lay a young sapling, stripped of its bark and limbs. "A heart," Hector said, "with an arrow through it."

Bonnie nodded.

"What is it for?" he asked.

"For me," she said. "But it didn't work."

Hector tried to read the reasons in her mind but couldn't begin to. With a shrug she turned and strode away, moving to the pickup as if she were angry.

"I'll tell you all about it sometime, if you want to hear," she said and started the pickup. She looked at Hector.

He nodded. "Yes," he said. "I would like to know. Sometime."

They drove back to the house in silence.

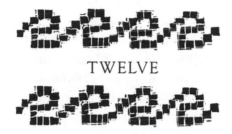

TWELVE

WITH STAKES AND STRING
Bonnie charted out a path for the rock walkway. Hector
followed behind, carefully cutting the brown turf, peel-
ing it back and laying it aside. He discovered that earth,
when it is freshly turned, smelled the same everywhere.
To him the smell was neither sweet nor sour, not like
that of fresh cut hay and not as strong as the manure of
cows or burros, but some place in between that he
found agreeable, even comforting.

Perhaps it was because the smell always took him
back to the first turned earth he knew, that of his
father's field. Hector's bare feet still knew the soft give
of that black, crumbly mountainside soil. He remem-

bered trying to stretch his steps to match those of his father's as he moved ahead and spoke softly to the oxen. The blade of the plow turned the earth aside like a wave on the great ocean to the west.

His father at first glanced back to see that he dropped the slick kernels of corn in the right way, bending each time so that the kernels wouldn't fall haphazardly but that the two he dropped would lie side by side, insuring that at least one would sprout.

Then with a sideways slide of his foot Hector would catch enough soil to cover the seeds and press it firm, deep enough to protect the seeds from crows and jays and to give them the darkness they needed to swell and burst with life. Then with a stick the length of both his father's feet he bent again and dropped two more kernels and then covered and then pressed. It was not unlike a dance, with a rhythm that soon was natural. Measure and bend and drop and cover and press. Soon his father stopped looking back and, although only six, Hector had become for the task of planting corn already a man.

Bonnie went to town for fine sand and mortar and the pickup crept back, swaying and groaning with its load. It took two days to cut and smooth the path so that it twisted and turned and circled just the way Bonnie wanted. Sometimes she stood and studied the design and then moved back and to one side to see it from another angle. The way it looked was important to her. Hector understood, for the weavers in Huitupan were the same, often more concerned with their designs than the strength of their garments.

For Hector a path was to go from one place to the next, and a man could just as well follow the way that a goat or a cow took each day in its own worn trail, for one would not find a better path. But he did not tell that to Bonnie.

The third day he spread the sand evenly into the paths and by the fourth day was ready to lay the rocks. With a hammer and chisel he knocked the uneven layers from the bottoms of the stones so that they would lie flat in the bed of sand. From a wheelbarrow of stones beside him he chose the ones that would fit, chipping here and there, turning each stone the way it was meant to go. For every place there was a right stone, if only you had the eye and the patience to find it.

At every turn of the path Hector sank small chips of stone in the soft mortar, their narrow edges up, to make a design — a bird or a star or a flower — and every two meters he ran a line of the same small chips in a double row across the width of the walk.

Before the sun set on Saturday the path was almost finished, lacking only a few more squares of stones that would join the paths to the doorways. Just before dark Bonnie came out to look.

"One more day and it will be complete," Hector said. He couldn't hide the pride in his voice.

Bonnie shook her head. "I can't believe how fast it went, and it's just the way I hoped it would be."

"So you are pleased?" Hector beamed. "When I finish

I will brush the joints of mortar smooth and wash the stones with water and when they dry, sweep them clean."

He looked over his work for a few moments and saw the small imperfections, a rock chipped too much, a low place in the center of one walk. "I could do better on another," he said, "for I have not laid rocks in many years."

"Well, maybe there will be another," Bonnie said with a wave of her hand. "It is so beautiful that maybe we'll just cover the whole yard with stone, and then who knows, maybe the whole world." She laughed then and took a sip from a fine and slender glass. *Vino blanco.* Hector could tell by the sweetness of its smell.

"But stop now," she said. "You've already worked too late. I'll bet you could use a beer." Then she pointed toward two metal chairs leaning backwards against the house. "Here," she said, "let's sit where we can admire the walk."

Hector looked at the wheelbarrow, the tools, his hands and arms, all splattered with half-dry mortar.

"I must clean my tools now, before the mortar dries," he said, "so that they will be ready for another day." He hesitated for a moment. "And I have no more beer."

"Oh my God, Hector," Bonnie said, and Hector could tell that she was in truth upset. "It's Saturday. I forgot. I'll bet you're out of everything." She hesitated a moment, looking at her wrist although she was not wearing a watch. "I just don't want to go to town again."

Then she became the *patrón* again, taking charge of everything, giving orders. "Hector," she said, "now don't worry about a thing. It's all my fault. You just clean up, and I'll take care of the beer. And the food, too."

Hector started to say that for something small like that he would never worry, and that he had food enough for one more night, and they had an agreement about the beer, but she didn't let him finish and before he could hardly move she was in and out of the house and handing him a cold Carta Blanca. "Now go, go," she said. "Give me twenty minutes, or maybe thirty, and we'll have supper, you know, *cena*. Okay?"

Yes, it was okay with Hector. It was good. The water from the shower was hot and at his feet ran gray and thick with sand and mortar and the foam of soap. His clothes lay clean and folded on his bed, a woman was preparing food for his evening meal, the Carta Blanca was not yet empty, and the night was Saturday, so that tomorrow was not a day for work. A very lucky man you have become, Hector Rabinal, he thought.

As he showered he began to hum a song, but it was the one that Leticia always sang to their boys as she bathed them under the sky of Huitupan. And so he stopped and tried to find another song, one of fiestas and harvests that are *grande*, but that song of bathing, a silly song that girls might sing to their sisters, would not leave his head.

For a few minutes Hector stood outside in the dark and waited. Bonnie had told him maybe thirty minutes and he did not want to be early. He watched as she moved in the kitchen, always in a hurry, opening the doors of cabinets, stirring something in a large pot, even sipping from her glass of wine, as if everything was one great race to be completed.

For the first time Hector saw her wearing a dress, long and white with many-colored flowers looping across the top and down the center. It was better than overalls.

When she placed the plates on the table Hector stepped to the door and said *hola*, softly at first and then again more loudly until she let him in with a little bow and the sweep of one arm and a soft and lilting laugh.

A fine meal. Much beer for Hector. He said no, but thank you when she offered him the wine. There was crusty bread much like *bolillos* and lettuce with tomatoes and a sauce that was lemony to his tongue, then long, flat pastas mixed with garlic, and crisp and broken bacon and tiny peas.

While they ate Bonnie asked and Hector told her about Leticia and Efrán and Tomasito, told her what was true about them, and about his brothers, and even about Father Cota, but as he talked Hector saw them all suspended in some strange place that was not Guatemala but also was not Mexico or anywhere else, but some place in his mind where he had placed them so that what he told Bonnie would not be a lie. He told her what was in his heart, which is always the truth, that he would send for his family and they would come to Texas and be with him, for that is what Father Cota said would be best.

"But how will they do that?" Bonnie asked. "They are Mexicans, like you, aren't they?"

"There will be no problem," Hector said, "for I will work hard and have many dollars and the bus will bring them the entire way."

"That's not exactly what I meant," Bonnie said, and for the first time Hector was not sure that he understood everything he should.

But right at that moment he was happy. He had a goal that he must work for, and he knew that the future did not always have to be completely seen or understood, for only a fool would think that.

Bonnie said no more about it, and while Hector sat and waited she took the dishes from the table, everything but the almost empty wine bottle and her glass.

Perhaps he should go, or would it be an insult, as in Huitupan, to leave too soon. But there was no way to compare, for Hector never would have eaten in the house of an unmarried woman there, for a woman would never live alone unless she were old and a *bruja* of some evil kind.

Bonnie brought coffee in heavy cups and with it two silver glasses without handles, each one small enough to hide in his closed hand. "Brandy," she said. "For the coffee. You know brandy?"

Hector took a small sip. "*Aguardiente*," he said. "No?"

"Close," she said and poured it into her coffee.

So in the same way, as if he did it every day, he poured the brandy into his cup.

Then Bonnie started talking, no longer with questions about Hector, but about herself, how she went to a university in the north, and afterwards there was a war. "The government said I was a bad woman," she said with a laugh. "So I went to Mexico, Cuernavaca for a while, then on down to Oaxaca." While she talked the silver bracelets slid up and down her arm and made the sound that bells on lost goats make from deep in the woods.

"You were alone," Hector asked, "and went to strange cities in Mexico?" For twenty years ago she would have been a señorita with smooth skin and golden hair that shone in the Mexican light and the men — no it would not have been possible..

"No," she said. "There was a man, more a boy as I remember him now."

"And he married you," Hector said.

"No," she laughed, "it wasn't like that."

Hector wanted to ask, then what could it have been like, to be a young and beautiful woman traveling and living all over a country other than your own with a man you were not married to. But he felt he must not ask that.

"Your family, then, your father and your mother, they did not know? They did not care?"

"They knew. And they cared in their own strange way, I guess. Oh, Hector, it sounds so weird when I try to explain it to you. It comes out sounding different and not like it was at all."

She poured the last of the wine into her glass and stared at the darkened window, but in the brightness of the room she could see nothing but herself.

128

Hector leaned forward in his chair. "Tell me then, for you said you would, about the giant heart of gravel. The one at the bottom of the canyon."

Bonnie brightened up at that, as if happy to leave where the other talk had taken her. "Well," she said, and looked at the empty bottle of wine and tilted her glass, just as empty, to one side. "Where do I start?" She slid the chair back and moved to the kitchen and returned with a half glass of wine.

"Well, like everything else in my life, this is complicated. But as simply as I can tell it, this is what happened. I met a man in Oaxaca some years ago — Zeke, short, you know, for the prophet. Anyway, Zeke was a poet of sorts or at least had the soul of a poet. Or at the very least was as discontented with America as I was."

"Discontent?" Hector asked.

"Yeah, you know, dissatisfied, unhappy."

"I know the word," Hector said, "but still I do not understand why this discontent."

"Complicated," she said. "The war, President Johnson, then Nixon." She could tell that Hector did not understand, that he had only wondered about the heart of gravel. To him discontent was what happened when your family was hungry or the military took your home from you. The discontent that she spoke of was to Hector harder to grasp than early morning fog in the valley of the mountains.

"Anyway," she said, and took a sip of wine. The bracelets jingled and she went on. "Zeke was a sweet fellow and we were both lost in the universe, so we hitched up."

"You married him?"

"It seemed the right thing to do at the time, and for a while it was okay. We settled down here in Laredo, always living on the border, on the edge, as Zeke would say. I got a little income when my parents died — I still do, enough to be comfortable, and Zeke kind of hung on here, going back and forth to L.A., you know, California."

Hector nodded.

"Zeke was always involved in this or that, the grape pickers, the lettuce growers, whatever, but nothing ever seemed to work out. Well, one day, not too many months ago, I said to myself, 'Bonnie, it's time you took charge of your life,' and I did. Oh, he talked and he promised and, under pressure, he even confessed to this and to that, none of which surprised me. But my mind was made up."

"And the heart of gravel?" Hector asked, for much that she had told him was too rapid and he did not fully understand, although it was clear from the way she spoke that Zeke did not treat her well, perhaps he drank too much brandy or was a lazy dog and would not work.

"Okay, the gravel heart." She looked at Hector softly, as if to say she was sorry for something that he could not know. "Well a few weeks ago, three or four before you showed up, Zeke stopped by. He drove me to the top of Devil's River Canyon, to just the place where you and I stopped, remember? And he led me to the edge. Well, let me tell you," she said with a little laugh and a sip and a jingle, "I didn't know what he had in mind. And to tell the truth, when I saw the heart — he had hired some bulldozer operator to make it, no telling what it cost — my own heart gave a little flutter. But I didn't give in, not one inch."

"And so the giant heart was a sign from him, that he still had love for you? And still you said no?"

"You would have had to be there, Hector, all those years, to understand."

Life for those who live in Texas must be very difficult, Hector thought, and he wondered if it was the same all over the United States, and if so would he always have to be in courtship to keep Leticia. He could never build giant hearts of gravel, and if even that would not work, then what was the use of being there.

The beer and the rich food and the brandy had softened his brain and it hurt to think more.

He thanked Bonnie for the time they had spent. She gave him a smile, a little bow, then extended her hand. Hector took it in his. Her fingers were long and her grip was smooth like fine fabric, but strong. To simply stand was not easy. He felt as if he were seeing the room from the edge of a cliff and the floor was swirling water, hiding rocks that could not be seen.

"You are okay?" Bonnie asked. "You poor thing. Beer and brandy don't mix very well, I guess."

But Hector told her he was fine. "Tonight," he said, and his voice echoed through the house, "is a night of fiesta, a celebration. For the stones of the path are almost all laid, and for the first time I will walk to my room without my feet touching the grass or the ground."

"Oh, not alone you won't!" And Bonnie grabbed his arm and walked with him, matching her steps to his. While they moved she hummed some song, like a processional, and at the entrance to his room sang, "da da da," the last sound rising in a kind of triumph. Then she whirled, her arms above her head and the silver bracelets caught the light of the moon like quick fish in a clear stream.

And then, and of this Hector was not sure, and even the next morning could not remember exactly. But after she twirled, in one quick and sudden movement he felt her body, the softness of her breasts, not bound at all, as they brushed against his arm and then his chest. And then, because the two of them were almost the same in height, her face swirled next to his and he smelled her hair, like a flowery vine that he had known. And then he tasted the sweet wine of her lips and felt the dew from the grape as it grazed his mouth.

Then she was gone, and the stars moved around the heavens as always, but hurrying somewhere Hector did not know, and his bed spun with them, carrying him to strange new places all through the night.

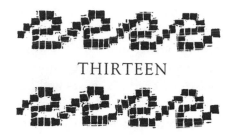

THIRTEEN

ALWAYS THERE WAS WORK
to do, some project that Bonnie wanted completed.
Hector watched and waited as she walked around the
yard on the new walk, stopping one place and then
another, always thinking and planning. She wanted gardens now, narrow ones that would follow the curves of
the rock walk.

It was December and there in that part of the country time to prepare gardens for planting. The weather
was different but not difficult for Hector to understand.
The wind from the north always blew cold, the wind
from the south always damp, the wind from the west
always dry. The wind never blew from the east, and

Hector awoke each morning to see if that would happen.

The wind from the south was Hector's favorite, for it blew across the charcoal and wood fires of Nuevo Laredo, where the women cooked tortillas on flat *copales* balanced on open fires or even tossed them on the hot coals and turned them with a quick poke and a twist of a green twig. From there drifted the trace of thin, charred slices of meat they had smeared with ground chiles and salt and the tart juice of *limones*. As Hector worked in Bonnie's yard the hint of that smoke touched his senses and he could see the women all over Mexico, and the women in Huitupan, and even Leticia, all squatting in their skirts of bright colors, fanning their small fires with one hand and turning tortillas lightly with the other, handing them to their daughters or mothers who brushed away the ash and stacked them.

While Hector turned the earth and picked out the small rocks and added the dried manure of sheep, Bonnie watched and she talked. She planned to plant flowers, mostly roses and daisies, in the sun, and other plants he did not know in the shade. One garden would have herbs, some that Hector had tasted many times — oregano, *yerba buena,* and basil — many others were new to him or had other names in Guatemala. Leticia would have known.

Hector asked for cilantro, and Bonnie agreed that, yes they should have much cilantro, but sown only a little at a time so that always there would be some that had not flowered. She knew much about growing plants, not corn and beans and squash like Hector did, and her ways were different from the ways he knew. But it was as if both of them felt the earth as part of themselves. Hector could tell by the way Bonnie took a handful of soil and squeezed it, to test the amount of *barro*, of clay, and the amount of sand it contained by the way it crumbled in her hand.

Some things were the same. When Hector walked through her small orchard he saw ribbons that hung from limbs of the trees, with small stones tied at the end of each one, so that the trees would be taught the way that ripe fruit would feel on their branches and they would bear heavily in the spring.

Some days Bonnie wore her white dress of many flowers and stayed away until late. Those were what she called her "Mexico days," days when she crossed the Rio Grande with her basket of woven straw, walking the long length of the bridge, and brought back small packages — thin candles wrapped in newspaper, tiny *milagros* for good fortune, always fresh flowers. Even a small *milagro* truck one day when her rose-colored pickup did not want to start.

Each day Hector watched as Bonnie walked out to the box at the side of the road to check for letters. Never had he seen so much mail. Never a day passed without a handful of brightly colored pamphlets, and periodicals, and official-looking letters. But so far, nothing for him.

Bonnie no longer took Hector to town on Saturdays.

It was not safe, she said. Not dangerous for him like it would have been in Chajul, for there his life would be taken in a moment, but the danger in Laredo was of being caught and found to be illegal, which he did not fully understand. For how could any man be illegal? All men were born the same, without the choice of where or at what time, and the world was so *grande* . . . how could a man not be legal?

Hector understood the laws, how they worked, why he must be careful, but he never understood *why* the laws were made and who approved them; as if there were invisible gods who sat in power and passed their wishes on men, but were blind and could never see if their laws caused them harm.

But Bonnie explained to him that the laws had changed, that there was now in the United States something called amnesty, which was a sort of forgiveness for being illegal. But only if you were illegal for the right length of time and for the right reasons and didn't try not to be illegal during that time or ever leave America to visit your family. It seemed to Hector that amnesty must be for only the worst of men.

So each Saturday Hector told Bonnie what he would need and she returned from the giant store with sacks of groceries and his money for the week. He felt he had no right to complain, although the times in the store had always given him small pleasures — the way the small children ran and slid on the slick floor or shyly hung on to their mothers, how the men talked and smoked their packages of cigarettes as they leaned against their pickup trucks. Then there was the discovery of strange new things that his money could buy.

Bonnie always asked if he wanted the chocolate cakes with cream inside and he always said no, even though that was not true. But for her to bring him cakes would be like a mother bringing candy to a child, and it made him angry, even a little at Bonnie, although he knew that was not right. She only tried to be generous, but perhaps she had forgotten how she should act toward a man.

It would be the time of Christmas soon, Bonnie told him, and on her Mexico days she brought small carved wooden animals painted in colors that animals never could be, and fine glass globes that sparkled when she unwrapped them in the sun.

She liked to show Hector what she had bought and, although he did not care much for such things, he welcomed the time, watching her as she described each small purchase, the way she looked and smelled, the way her voice at those times rang high and clear and excited like that of a young girl. She was very beautiful at those times and watching her, being close to her, was a small gift in his life and one that he accepted gratefully.

One night — it was a Friday and almost the day of Christmas — Bonnie was in town until late and when she came home Hector watched from his room as the lights of her house began to come on. The glow of the tree of Christmas sparkled against the window of one dark room and music, some full of life, some slow and sad, filled the night.

It had been the same every night that week. Hector lay back down on his bed in the dark and listened to the songs, trying to understand more each time he heard them, but the words were soft and blended together like wool on a loom, and it was not easy to do.

Hector was almost asleep when a car door slammed at the side of the house. Then he heard footsteps going to the back, at first almost indistinct on the soft ground, and then, when they found the stone walk, hard and heavy, and Hector could tell they were the boots of a man.

The man did not knock, did not say a word that Hector could hear, but the kitchen light flashed on. Bonnie had heard him, too. Perhaps she had been waiting for him. Hector stood then in the dark of the room and watched. Bonnie was wrapped in a white *rebozo* that covered all but her feet. She was not wearing shoes. The man was not heavy at all, but slender, much the same as Hector, so his steps must have been taken in anger to have been so loud.

Hector could not understand his words, but every time he stopped talking, Bonnie said "No." Finally she let him in and Hector watched quietly, hidden by the dark. Bonnie sat, then stood, and her arms waved as she talked. Her voice was loud and then soft and then loud again. Then his voice was loud and hers was louder, then his the loudest of all and Hector was afraid that he might hit her. But he stood with his arms folded while Bonnie moved around the room as if it were a cage.

Finally he left, slamming the door behind him, and Bonnie followed him into the dark. The moon was only a small hard ball that night, but it was enough for Hector to see the white of her *rebozo*. It flashed with tiny sparkles as she moved, opening a little with each step. Her legs were long and white, and her feet slapped the rock walk like hands shaping wet clay.

He heard voices again, hers and then the man's. The sounds rose together, then fell together, as if they were singing an old song they both knew very well.

Then an engine roared to a start and lights flashed on and tires spun on gravel, and the man was gone.

For a few minutes Hector heard nothing, and he wondered if Bonnie had left with him, but he had heard only one door of the car slam shut. So he stood in the stillness of his room and listened.

Then from the shadows of the trees he heard Bonnie again. It was as if she were chanting and at first Hector thought she might be casting some secret spell upon the man. Soon he heard her steps, each one so hard that it must have stung the soles of her feet, and the chant became louder, each step and each word in perfect rhythm.

"Damnhim, damnhim, damnhim." The chant was heavy and forceful, and without thinking Hector took a step back from the window as she passed closer.

"Damnhim, damnhim, damnhim." Again and again, over and over, until the words became a cry and the cry became a wail, not unlike that of a wolf, lonely and hungry, howling at the side of a barren mountain. "Oooh, oooh, damnhim!"

The door to the kitchen slammed again and she disappeared. The house went dark again and for a moment the night was still and quiet. Then from the kitchen Hector saw the small light of the refrigerator, which comes on like magic when it opens. Then off again. It was closed.

Then the light of a match, and then the light of a candle and then another and another. First the kitchen, then the other rooms of the house began to glow with candles, and it seemed, but for the softness of the glow, that the whole house might be afire.

After a few minutes Hector lay back down, and for awhile he listened but could hear nothing else. The man in the car might return, he thought, and he waited for the sound of that engine which he would know again.

After some time his mind spun off to that place of half-sleep where thoughts are not quite dreams, yet dreams have escaped from thoughts, and stayed there until he fell into a deep sleep.

Then, as if it were in a dream, Hector heard his name softly called. And for a few moments he enjoyed the softness of the voice, the feeling that someone might call to him in the night, for it had been so long.

Then the voice again. "Hector, please," and he awoke with a start. Bonnie was outside his door.

He slipped on his clothes and went out. She was waiting for him, still all in white, and she motioned for him to go with her. She was holding a glass shaped like a globe, and as he got closer he smelled the brandy. She offered the glass to him and he hesitated, then started to speak, to ask if there was anything he could do, if she was hurt in some way. But she put her finger to his lips to silence him and shook her head as if in answer to the questions he had never asked.

Hector followed her into the house and then from room to room. She would stop before each group of candles and take a sip of brandy. She offered it to Hector and blew out the candles one at a time, as if it were some kind of ceremony. Hector took the brandy and sipped slowly. It was as if she were a shaman and the brandy were *posh* and would cure whatever might be wrong.

She left the candles in her bedroom burning, and their smoke had the sweetness of ripe fruit and delicate flowers, and the walls gleamed with the shimmer of silver *milagros*. Music from another room floated low and sad in the air, music of a people who had no home, who must wander the world forever. People much like what Hector had become.

The brandy and the music made Hector lonely, but for what he was not certain, for at that moment he did not want to be with Leticia or with his brothers or with his children. The loneliness was like a hunger that he did not want to hurry away with a table of rich food, but wanted to savor as he slowly nibbled.

Then Bonnie turned to him and spoke one word. "Dance?" And when Hector started to say that he did not know her way to dance she put a finger to his mouth a second time to silence him. That was the only word she spoke that night, and then only once. "Dance?"

She held him and they moved. Hector did not know what to do, but it did not matter. Bonnie led him around the room to that music of wanderers and to the spin of silver *milagros*. The floor was smooth. Their feet slid together, and they circled the room again and again until the music stopped.

She gently pushed Hector away and he stood still and watched. It was like a dream. She whirled in a small circle, sweeping her head to one side. Her eyes were the eyes of a *bruja* who had fallen under a spell of her own making.

Her skin was white where the *rebozo* began to unwind, and the candles went out, one at a time, as she moved past them. She whirled and whirled and stumbled once and the smallest of laughs escaped from her.

Then it was dark except for the light from the small moon, and she moved close to him again. For a moment she was still, then Hector felt her fingers on his shirt and it was open and then off. She took his hands and moved them gently to her breasts and Hector held each one as if they were the finest fruit and not to be bruised.

Her *rebozo* slipped to the floor and her hands were at his belt and Hector felt himself strain tight against his trousers, and then he was loosed and grew in the cool of the room, and the bed was softer than the down of many birds and her hands had the sureness and strength of a potter. Her mouth was warm and wet like the lowlands of the coast, her breath flowed from a hot spring, and between her legs the dampness lay dark and fertile, like a secret place deep in the forest where leafy ferns sprout and sway.

The light from the moon grew larger, then was gone. The night went forever and would never end, then it, too, was gone.

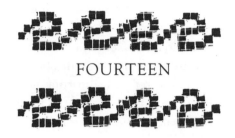

FOURTEEN

HECTOR had never heard the expression, "back to business," until Bonnie used it the next day. But he understood it from Bonnie's way of talking and moving, the way her words only told him of the work to be done; the way she would one moment look him right in the eye as if challenging him in some way and at other times keep her eyes away from his while she talked, often for several strained minutes.

But then there were other that day , while Hector wheelbarrowed leftover rocks to a back-field pile, that he could feel Bonnie's stare as he moved, and its intensity burned through him.

But she didn't mention their night together, and after

a few days Hector began to wonder if it had really happened, or if his desperate need had just driven his imagination over a Devil's River Canyon that had hidden in his mind.

On Christmas Day Hector had not planned to work and got up later than usual. Bonnie's pickup was already gone when he stepped out into the gray damp cool of the morning. At his door he found a bright green package with a note that listed a number of small jobs for him to do and asked him to water her indoor plants and to please bring in the mail. She was spending a few days with her sister in California and wished him a Merry Christmas. At the end of the note, big swirling loops of red ink said, "Affectionately, Bonnie."

The box held a new hat, not one for work, but one made of black felt with a tiny red feather in its brim.

"Affectionately, Bonnie." The words circled through his mind all day long and followed a rhythm of their own. He repeated them over and over aloud, and those words, "Affectionately, Bonnie," were everywhere. They bounced off the roof as he tossed down fallen branches and stiff patches of dried leaves. The words thumped up from his feet as he walked along the rock path. What did they mean, he wondered. How much affection was in "affectionately"? Or was that the same as using "Dear" to write to anyone, even a stranger, in a letter?

Hector knew it was the day of Christmas, but he worked anyway, unable to sit still for more than a moment. Even while he ate his midday meal he paced back and forth in his tiny house. He carried a cold piece of chicken in one hand and wore his new black hat, stopping before the bathroom mirror for a few moments each time, hardly able to believe that it was Hector Rabinal he was seeing.

The days crept along. Hector watered Bonnie's plants, moving from room to room, and ended up standing by the soft bed for many minutes, trying once again to bring back all that had happened on that one magical night.

He tried to envision what it might be like to live in that house with her, to sit in any one of five different rooms, to have a giant fan in the attic to pull cool wind through with the silent touch of a switch. He wanted to sleep in the bed, hoping that its smell and its softness would bring everything back, but he dared only to sit on its edge. Later, he carefully brushed the little ripples of wrinkles from its cover, gently, as if he were smoothing Bonnie's soft skin.

Three days after Christmas, in the afternoon mail, tucked in the fold of the colored splash of a supermarket flyer, Hector found a letter addressed to him. At first he could not believe it, and for a few minutes he sat at Bonnie's kitchen table with her growing stack of mail in front of him and simply stared at the words.

B. Cota was printed in the upper left corner along with a post office address in Comitan, Chiapas, Mexico. Hector's name was written in Father Cota's familiar hand, and he felt a rush of loneliness and strangeness and guilt surge through him.

A part of him wanted to bury the unopened letter

deep in the soft soil of the garden where it would rot and never be seen by anyone. He even felt angry at the letter's intrusion into his life there, a life with good work and fair wages and a solid house and safety — and a life he could share with Bonnie.

Just seeing Father Cota's name plunged him back part way into his other life, one that he had covered and smeared with all that was new until it could no longer be clearly seen or heard or even felt.

But finally he had to read it:

Hector, My friend, My son,

I had been away from Altomirano, on a mission that I will relate later, so your letter had been here several days when I returned. From its contents I assume that you had not received my letter of August 2, which I sent to you via air mail in care of Señor Tiemann's address.

So I must relate once again the news of that undelivered letter and, also again, relive the pain it must cause us both.

I will start from the beginning and tell what I know, although the truth of those few days in Huitupan may never be revealed completely.

After you defended your home from the two soldiers, you saw Leticia and Tomasito and Efrán disappear into the woods. They surely were, as you guessed, headed for Todos Santos and the safety of Adolfo's home. But, and for this part of the story we must rely on what Tomasito has been able to tell us, another group of three soldiers apparently had seen them as they ran. After the second group of soldiers emptied from the truck and found their mutilated comrades, most began to chase after you, but the three others followed your family into the woods.

Then it is all the account of Tomasito and we must remember that even now he has only six years and the events of those hours were beyond his full comprehension. But, evidently, the three soldiers caught up to them within only a kilometer or two, for the next morning an old man from Pizayal herding his goats through the fresh undergrowth came upon the two boys shivering and lost. He fed them goat's milk warm from the udder and both now are healthy, but in some way Tomasito had lost most of the vision in one eye, probably from a fall in the night. His sight in that eye has not fully returned and may never. It is out of our hands.

Your brothers and cousins, and everyone that was left (some also without homes, for the soldiers destroyed many) searched the woods for days, but Leticia has not been found. Tomasito told of a fight between the soldiers and his mother and how one soldier took the boys away through the trees until they could no longer see her. He threw them to the ground and told them not to move. Then he left and they were alone. Tomasito heard Leticia's screams for a few minutes and tried to go toward the sounds, but then all became quiet and he could not find her, so the two boys wandered in the denseness of the woods until they fell exhausted. They cried until luckily they were found.

Tomasito cannot remember hearing a gun discharge

nearby, so perhaps Leticia has been taken to some prison, or she could have escaped and be hiding in a nearby village, afraid to come out, for everything is different. Huitupan is no more.

I just returned from there, a journey that was full of danger, but I had to see for myself, with my own eyes, in order to believe what senseless cruelty men can inflict upon their brothers.

The homes of a few scattered families remain, spared only because they could not be easily found. Everything else is gone. Only the land remains, and the terraces of the fields are eroding badly with no one to tend them, and the ashes of the houses have turned the stream in the valley to the color of darkness.

Your brothers Pascual and Mendez have become the leaders of your people now. They have settled across the border in Mexico, just to the south of Comitan, at a camp where they are safe. Pascual has taken the boys and is caring for them like his own, but it is not easy.

Perhaps my advice to you, to go to the north, was not right, and for that I ask your understanding and forgiveness. For we are neither all-knowing nor all-seeing and both know that you would still be here if we had imagined what would have occurred.

I do not need to tell you that you are needed. I know you will come when this reaches you. In the old days I would have wished you the speed of God, but now it seems that God can deliver only evil, so I wish you good health and a safe journey.

Bartolo Cota

For a day and a night Hector could hardly move. His bed became a prison that would not release him. What Father Cota had written constantly stirred to life in his mind, and over and over again he watched as Leticia enters the woods with the boys.

But it doesn't stop with that. He sees them scrambling across the side of the mountain, Leticia slipping as she carries Efrán, Tomasito struggling to keep up, Leticia pleading with them both not to cry, but their small voices ricochet through the canyons, leading the soldiers to them.

Then one of the brownshirts wrenches Efrán from Leticia, and grabs Tomasito, and with both boys struggling in his arms disappears into the gloom of the woods.

The other two throw Leticia to the ground and brutally take their revenge on the wife of their comrades' killer. Over and over again. And then it is dark and Leticia has disappeared as if she were a ghost and Hector, in the fever of his imagination, cannot find her.

But the boys wander until dark and still will not stop. Tomasito chases after Efrán who keeps running away and falls into a bush of thorns, and his sight is now cut in half and he gives up and hugs his brother until morning, rocking and crying and holding his eye.

Then the old man finds them and pulls the warm milk of a ewe into their mouths and they drink greedily and thankfully as if it were from their mother's breast.

It was his dream when he slept and his dream when awake. For a day it never left him and he could not move from his bed. Always he was a witness who must watch. It was his punishment and he could not escape it.

Bonnie returned to a man she did not know. Hector had slept and tossed and sweated in his clothes for three days. He had not eaten. His eyes had grown dark and appeared to be hidden deep in his skull.

"You are sick?" she asked, and he simply handed her the letter. As she read it her face took on the hurt and pain that Hector felt. She shook her head slowly, from side to side as she read, able only to murmur "Oh, no, oh, no," every few words.

While he gathered his things together, Bonnie prepared food for his journey and found for him a shirt and some blue jeans from her closet. They didn't talk for there was nothing to say. When she stuffed his final dollars into his pocket, he didn't care enough to count them.

Finally, Bonnie told him, "You can always come back. There will be a place for you here."

But Hector shook his head. "My place should never have been here. I was so wrong. So wrong." And his face darkened even more, and he wanted not to be a man but to be a small boy again, so that he could start everything over once more, and so that he could cry and from somewhere receive the softness of familiar comfort. For he was afraid and wanted not to be afraid of the unknown he would find at Huitupan, afraid for Leticia and her sons, and, yes, desperately afraid for himself.

Bonnie could not give that comfort, for what reasons he never did know. All she could do was pat his arm twice, then again, and give a tiny squeeze. Perhaps she felt a part of his guilt, thinking that she had held him there for her own reasons and helped keep his dream alive when she knew that it never could be.

Hector closed his eyes when Bonnie touched his arm and told himself that he wanted no more. But that was not right, and he knew it. He wanted more at that moment than he could have ever dreamed but would have refused had she somehow been able to offer it.

Then Bonnie stepped back and said she would take him to town, but he said no.

"Hector," Bonnie said. "I'm sorry. I'm really sorry for everything."

"Today," Hector said, "I can feel nothing but a sadness that has layered itself inside of me like a wall made of thin, jagged rocks. Today it is only right to be sorry and to be sad, but tomorrow will be different for both of us."

And with that Hector stepped back a few slow steps, and stopped, looking at Bonnie. Then with deliberateness he turned and headed to the south.

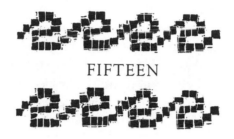

FIFTEEN

IF YOUR SKIN IS BROWN and
you travel to the south no one cares. At midday, Hector
stripped and waded the Rio Grande just west of Laredo,
balancing everything he owned on his head with one
hand. The water was thick and brown and cool, and he
hurried to dress again on the other side, shivering under
the wind-churned clouds overhead.

The buses were not so crowded on the way back, and
the mood of the passengers more subdued, as if the fiesta they had come to attend was over and now it was
time to return to the dailiness of their lives.

Hector slept all that he could. He had divided his
money into three stacks. Most he put deep in his sock at

155

the back of a boot; another, smaller stack of bills, he folded once longways and hid in the flap inside the brim of his new felt hat. The rest he shoved deep in one pocket and that is what he pulled out for food as he traveled.

The buses were all the same. They swayed and roared and rocked and screeched and sped down through the country as if driven by madmen. They smelled of sour fruit and urine and sick babies and beer. The passengers moved in and out at stops, yet all were the same. Some sat beside Hector and talked, but he heard little and understood nothing. Their faces and their shifting bodies changed, and Hector neither noticed nor cared.

He slept with his hat gripped across his chest by night and tilted across and hiding his face by day. His world became one continuous dream with many different endings, a dream that he could never change. Always there was Leticia with her screams. Sometimes Hector saved her, with superhuman strength pulling the brownshirts away and tossing them to the side like dry bundles of cane. But the next time he would be unable to move, as if his feet were deep into an earth that was made of glue, and he could do nothing but watch and finally scream, and then awaken when the faceless person next to him gave him a slap across the arm.

At Huajuapan the bus stopped and idled while passengers slid by each other in the aisle. Outside, Hector watched a woman dressed in red holding a baby. The baby kept pushing on her lap with its feet and arching its back and waving its tiny arms as if it were a baby bird almost ready to fly. While the baby pushed and bounced the woman stared back at Hector with a quizzical look on her face, and just as the bus drew away, she pulled open the front of her dress, exposing one heavy brown breast, and when the baby found her nipple, she gave Hector a smile.

At those short stops vendors thrust their wares at the open windows. There were plastic bags of drinks of many colors stuck with striped straws, and *buñuelos* dripping with honey, and slices of melons. Hector chose carefully, knowing that money might never again be so easy to get.

At Comitan Hector stepped down stiffly from the bus. Guatemala could be no more than a hundred kilometers south — his boys were somewhere close by, exactly where, Father Cota would tell him. In the market he caught a *colectivo* that took him through chalky rolling hills to Altomirano.

For two days Hector told his story to Father Cota, holding back nothing, reaching back into his memory for details that had before escaped him. Father Cota listened closely, stopping him often to clarify an event or to ask what was in his heart at this or that time.

Father Cota seemed to have gained many more years in the few months since Hector had seen him. He no longer moved quickly like a young man but had sunk into himself and often sat for hours in one place, getting up only with painful effort.

When Hector's story was complete and he had slept and eaten from the kitchen of Father Cota's cousin, the two men eased out of the house and made their way to the church. There Father Cota once again arranged candles across the pine-needled floor, this time with different colors, more orange and yellow and a blue that was almost black. This ceremony was simpler. Father Cota had an assistant, a young man, who had been born with the gift and was training to become a shaman, and he chanted and passed the *posh* while Father Cota stood and stared upward with his eyes half-closed.

Once in the cleansing ceremony Father Cota whispered something to his assistant and then joined Hector who had knelt on the hard-packed floor, for even a shaman must fight against the darkness that is everywhere, even within his own soul. The two men joined hands and raised them up, holding them there while their voices joined together in the floating smoke of the room.

Afterwards, back at the house, Father Cota told Hector how to find San Caralampio, a *campamento* south of Comitan where Pascual and his wife cared for Tomasito and Efrán.

In the Comitan market Hector found a vendor of hats and traded his black felt hat, the Christmas gift from Bonnie, for the sturdy straw one of a *campesino*. With the extra money from the exchange Hector purchased a machete, one that was worn, but made of a heavier steel than the new ones. Its blade had been ground to a sharpness that only fine blades could hold. He found a sheath of tanned cow hide decorated with strings of leather fringe and the machete slid smoothly into it up to its handle as if they had been made by the same hands.

San Caralampio lay east of the main road that led to the Guatemalan border. The way to it was hardly more than a rocky trail, too rugged for *colectivos* or buses to traverse, so Hector walked the five kilometers in from the highway. On the way, fields of last year's corn stubble spread out in a fertile valley that ran north and south. But the surrounding land rose up and flattened out as plateaus of rocky outcroppings. The few twisted trees that Hector saw ahead of him clung to the upland strata of rocks like the last survivors from another age.

As he moved to the east Hector began to see the first houses of San Caralampio on a rise above him. They were squatty squares made of dried stalks of cane with flaps of tar paper or tin for doors. As he got closer and the trail became steeper, the ground under his boots turned to sheaths of red rock. The houses sat starkly on the land, as the ground around them would not support even a single flower, much less a small garden or field. For there was no soil; it had washed and blown and drifted to the valley centuries before.

Among the strangers that peered out of their fragile houses, Hector finally saw a familiar face or two, and small children soon raced in every direction, spreading the news that Hector Rabinal was back.

In a few minutes Hector spotted a crowd coming toward him, Pascual leading the way at a trot. As he embraced his younger brother his eyes searched through the faces for Leticia, but she was not there. Then others, Rafael, his cousin, and then two nephews and an aunt who rocked up to him on her bad leg. Few women were there and when Hector asked why, Pascual told him that they were all at the village well, each waiting to fill her two jars that would have to last the day. For there was only enough water underground to run the pump for thirty minutes each morning.

"Leticia is there, with the other women?"

Pascual shook his head and took Hector's arm. "Come, you must see your boys and then we can talk."

Tomasito had been exploring a cave nearby and heard the news late, but when he did, he came running and with a leap was in Hector's arms, his legs locked tightly around his father's waist. Hector could say nothing, just rock the boy from side to side. Finally he sat Tomasito down and knelt in front of him. "Let me see that eye," Hector said, and taking his hat, shaded the boy's face. The right eye was bright and as brown as a cacao seed, but the other one had a milkiness to it that floated like a high thin cloud.

"I can see all there is to see with this one," Tomasito said, for he sensed Hector's disappointment and fear.

Hector could only hold him close once again, until Tomasito squirmed away and ran off with a friend, eager to get back to the cave.

"And Efrán? Is he here?" And Hector searched the crowd of faces once more.

Then he saw Adelina, the wife of Pascual. She stood at the side of a nearby house holding Efrán. The boy was thin and the brown of his skin had turned almost yellow.

"Since he came here he has been sick," she said. "The water, perhaps, or because Leticia is not here. Who can know?"

"Do you have a shaman?" Hector asked. "Or is there a doctor who could come from Comitan? One who knows what to do."

"Once we had a little medicine and it seemed to help, but it is gone. And Father Cota no longer can make the trip here more than once in a few weeks. We do what we can, but there is nothing here in this place, even for the teas that we made in Huitupan."

Hector moved close to Adelina who, despite everything, had the familiar purple ribbons braided into the blackness of her hair. He started to take Efrán from her, to hold him, but the boy only stared vacantly past him as if he had never before seen his father.

"This will not do," Hector said. "We cannot live this way." Then he turned to Pascual. "Do you have fields to work? Why are the men not in the fields?"

"The only land we have is this." And Pascual waved his arm around to take in the rocky hill.

"When I walked in, there were fields with deep soil for corn and beans and squash on both sides of the road."

"Oh, we work in those fields," Pascual responded, "and, yes, the ground is rich, but the land belongs to a man who lives in San Cristobal and his foreman needs us only for planting and for harvest, and for that we are paid not much more than children. The Mexicans do not want us here. They fear for their own jobs, and they guard like gold the importance they have with their *patróns*. They will start to plant next month, and need us then, but for now all we can do is wait."

"We will leave, then," Hector said. "I have been from the south to the north of Mexico and it is a huge country. There will be other places where we can again have the chance to live as we did in Huitupan."

"There is no way," Pascual said, and Hector could see that his eyes were those of a man who no longer could imagine past that one day. "The Mexicans, their military, will not let us leave. We even hear rumors that we will be sent back to Guatemala or relocated in some place to the south that is worse, with only swamps and more disease. We are better off to stay here and take what little is given."

Then they went to Pascual's house and sat on the rough rock that was the floor while Adelina heated tortillas on the small coals. Hector refused to eat, to take when there was so little. He stared at Efrán who lay listlessly in one corner and thought back with guilt to the supermarket in Texas, with its rows and rows of food, and how he had wanted Bonnie to bring him just those things that he had learned to like the best, and how he had felt a small anger, like that of a spoiled child, when she forgot something.

"And what of Huitupan?" Hector asked. "Is it as bad as Father Cota has told me?"

"You would not recognize the village of our father." Pascual tapped ashes from a tortilla as he talked. "We hear the government will resettle it with those who they consider loyal, for the land is too rich to sit idle.

But we were not disloyal, for all we wanted was to farm the land that was ours. We didn't care about all the rest, for the beans and the squash and the corn are the same, not caring who sits the highest in the capital."

"And what of Leticia?" Hector asked. And he knew when the words came from him that he had been waiting a long time to ask that question. "Has there been any other word?"

"Nothing." Pascual looked at the ground as he answered, and Adelina poured water from a small bowl and began to bathe Efrán carefully, wiping the small ridges of his body with short, gentle strokes. The boy did not make a sound.

"What do you think has happened to her? You are my brother. You must be truthful with me."

"The only truth that I can tell you, my brother, is that no one can know. Perhaps the truth will be found, for she may be somewhere still alive." And then he paused a moment. "But the more time that passes with no word, the darker her chances seem to be."

Then Pascual felt that there was no more to be said about Leticia, that he had no way to help his brother, so he asked Hector about his adventure to the north. Hector's story wound around the room for hours, finding its way from Hector's heart and flowing to his brother. When he came to the part about Bonnie, Adelina left the room as if to honor the closeness of the two men.

"Was it hard, then, for you to come back?" Pascual asked. "To leave the house with hot water and much food and a beautiful *patrón?*"

"Not as hard as it would have been to stay," Hector answered, and Pascual nodded as if, yes, he understood. And to him Hector was the same man who had left, an older brother whom he had always followed after. And he saw that that would not change.

Pascual moved across the small room and dug around in a pile of blankets. When he came back he pulled a wooden cork from a jug shaped from red clay. He passed it to Hector. "This I told Adelina I would not taste until you returned."

Then he said, "And I thought you never would. Drink my brother." He laughed like they were boys again, and that laugh was the first that Hector had heard in all his hours of being in San Caralampio.

The brothers drank and felt the past year begin to rebuild itself, like a bridge of vines stretching over a steep mountain stream.

That night, while the rest of them slept — Pascual and Adelina and their three girls and Tomasito and Efrrán — all stretched out across the floor, almost filling the whole room under the thinness of old blankets, Hector roamed the rugged hill of rock and finally felt the night open up before him.

There was only one thing to do. It was so simple he wondered why it had never occurred to him before.

In the house he stepped among the sleepers. Pascual stirred. Hector found Efrán and then Tomasito and lay between them holding both until a gray light began to seep among the straw of the roof. Then, without a word, he left.

164

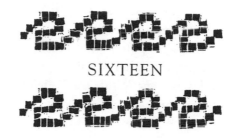

SIXTEEN

TO FIND LETICIA was the key. In the night the clarity of that solution had over-whelmed Hector with its suddenness. With Leticia back little Efrán would respond and heal from whatever he suffered. She would know the poultices and ointments to use on Tomasito's eye. And Leticia would be able to smooth away the memory of Bonnie and all that he had seen in the north.

For even as Hector moved swiftly up from the low-lands of Mexico and began to climb toward the moun-tains that signaled the Guatemalan border, his mind moved from inventing ways of searching for his lost, by now almost ephemeral wife, to recalling the smell of

Bonnie's hair and the tiny drops of sweat that formed above her lips when she worked beside him.

The second day he knew that he had crossed into Guatemala, although he was far from any road or any sign. Somehow the air had a feel that was familiar, whether from the altitude or the mix of woods that mingled in the smoke rising from the roofs of scattered houses he didn't know. Perhaps he had become like some migrating bird that could not help but respond to the invisible pull of what had been always its home.

From a goatherd's wife he bought a stack of tortillas and some eggs. While she boiled them he drank a cup of the morning's warm thick milk. The woman talked to him as if he belonged there, the sound of her words those of his father's. He had almost forgotten who he was, that he was not a Mexican and not an illegal, but a man of the Guatemalan mountains, and at that moment he knew that they were his home.

Pascual and Father Cota both had told Hector that the men of Huitupan had searched for Leticia, and he did not doubt that as the truth. But also he knew that panic had surely spread throughout the village when the soldiers came and even the best intentioned of men, even his own brothers, would have looked out first for the lives of their own families.

So it was a matter of being more systematic, more careful. He would search the woods first, all the way to Todos Santos, if necessary. The secret places of caves and trees and deep gullies he knew like a young man knows the smooth neck of his lover.

If he found no trace of her there, then he would work from house to house, then village to village, moving in an ever-widening circle out from Huitupan. Somehow he would find her. Then . . . and there Hector stopped, for he could not clearly see any farther.

But what if he found that she had died at the soldiers' hands? At that thought he walked faster, slamming each step to the ground to punish himself for the dream that slipped into his mind. For he knew that without Leticia the *campamento* at San Caralampio would never do for him or for his sons. And he despised the part of him that secretly wished for it to be so.

For he knew that without Leticia the three of them would go to Laredo. They could ride a bus almost all of the way, for Hector still had a thick fold of dollars in his boot. Bonnie would know the right doctors there and soon Efrán would be running in the aisles of the giant stores and Tomasito's eye would be healed. Hector could work for Bonnie and perhaps they could all live in her big house together. All things were possible in America.

And if he found Leticia hiding in some *campesino's* remote hut deep in a forgotten canyon? Then what? That possibility dropped across his shoulders like a load of green wood, and his mind scattered this way and that with the possibilities. Perhaps Leticia would go with them. They could all live together, and Leticia could cook and care for the boys. Bonnie would like her, for she was a gentle woman and not quick to show her anger. Hector could love them both, for in truth he did, each in a different way.

But then Hector would shout out loud, where all the trees and rocks he passed could hear, "Hector Rabinal, you have become a fool!" For he knew that Leticia would not go, and even if she did, that Bonnie would laugh at him for dreaming such a crazy dream.

Hector moved more cautiously as he approached Huitupan, fighting an impulse to hurry, for he had been walking for four days and was eager to arrive. But he rested at the edge of the woods until almost dark, the same woods that bordered his orchard, the same woods that had hidden him so well from the soldiers when he had fled. He felt comfortable there and watched quietly. He could see the small village plaza in the valley below, but it seemed deserted. Many of the houses that he remembered were only flat black spots on the earth. He thought he could see smoke trailing from a house or two that still stood, but in the gray of the evening he could not be sure.

His house was all but gone. Only one half of a wall stood black against the cliff behind it. Hector's two-wheel cart still sat tilted next to the ruin of the house. The rains had washed much of the ash down the hill leaving the debris to bleach in the sun. It seemed as if no one could have lived there for years.

The fields had grown up in weeds and small sprouts of trees, and the terraces had small rivulets where they had eroded and not been repaired. It hurt Hector to see his land so neglected. But, at least, no one else was working it. Perhaps the soldiers would not return, and the land could be reclaimed. Perhaps there was a new government in the capital, and they had passed their own laws of amnesty. It could be, he thought, but no, Father Cota surely would have known.

Right at dark he skirted the orchard, staying in the edge of the woods, then boldly strode across the open field to the remains of his house.

Someone had evidently searched through the ashes, for Hector could find almost nothing. In one corner the giant *comal* that had held so many tortillas lay split like a shattered star. Kicking around in the debris he found the charred box that had held Leticia's wedding necklace and the brightly colored dress that her mother had woven for that sacred day. But it was empty. Could Leticia have slipped back after the fire and taken them?

Hector was relieved when it was too dark to see more. This was the house that he and his brothers had built so solidly with their own hands, with clay from the side of the hill and limbs from the woods that surrounded him. And now, for Hector to see that house reduced to no more than a worthless pile caused a great sadness to sweep through him. He could feel the sadness begin, knew where it came from and fought against it, but it was as unstoppable as a spring waterfall.

Hector fell to his knees in the dark middle of what had been his house. He took great double handfuls of ash and dirt and held them to his face, then tossed them up and let them fall over him like the soft after-rain of a volcano. He did this over and over again until he was immersed with the remains of his house and his moans swept softly through the valley.

Then he found the old familiar path down to the stream. There he stripped and lay in the shallow rushing water, then waded out to a deep pool where he dived to the bottom.

Later, in the shallows of the stream, he carefully washed his clothes, rinsing the coating of sand and ash from them in the same way he had cleansed his clothes of blood months before. Tomorrow he would be ready to begin the search for Leticia.

He put on the pants and shirt that Bonnie had given him and hung his wet clothes across the brambles of a low bush. He lay down where the sound of the stream rushed through his mind and kept the rest of the night from entering. Then he slept.

The next day he felt the sureness of his plan begin to weaken. With the noise of the stream so near he could hear none of the valley's sounds that he remembered. No chickens squabbling or burros complaining or the yelping and scuffling of dogs. There were no cries of play or impatience from children. Nothing but the swirl and rush as the water churned and curved and cut its way down the mountain.

It was as if, in filling his ears with the constancy of the water, he had lost his sense of hearing. He felt vulnerable and even weak and a time or two had to fight off a panic that descended upon him, one that urged him to run to the shelter of the woods once more and find his way back to San Caralampio.

The story of what he would tell took shape in his mind, how he had searched the thicket all the way to

Todos Santos, how he found some bones, but could not tell if they were Leticia's. How he could never find another sign. How he talked to the scattered few who remained secluded in their mountainside huts and how they silently looked at one another and shrugged, either being ignorant or afraid to talk to him, since the informers for the soldiers could be anyone and anywhere. He finally gave up and returned to get his sons, his imaginary story went, to take them to the north where they could be treated and made well again. No one could find fault with that. No one would ever know.

But even as the story spun through his head he made his way back up the steep rise to the ruin of his house. Behind it, up against the sheer cliff that gave it shelter, he made his camp. From there the sounds that he knew so well came back to him and somehow he felt whole and restored. Again his plan to find Leticia seemed inevitable. To prove that his newfound spirit was real and existed not only in his imagination, he built a small fire with charred limbs from his house and watched the smoke rise and curl, clinging to the side of the cliff, announcing to anyone who might look that way that Hector Rabinal had returned to find his wife. And perhaps to reclaim his land.

For as he looked out over the terraces of his fields he felt a need rise deep from within him, one as basic as his need for a woman, one that urged him to find a pair of oxen and a plow of seasoned hardwood and once again turn the soil. It was that time of year.

While he waited for the fire to turn to coals he cleared a smooth place nearby with the scrape of his boot. Then he squatted to brush it smooth and with a stick outlined the valley of Huitupan and the woods that ran down the mountain to Todos Santos. This would be the map that would guide him. The stream became a snake-like groove in the sand. Along either side Hector filled in the houses, aware that some would no longer be there, then the village itself with its *parque* that contained the tiny gazebo. There he had played Sunday afternoons as a young boy, while his parents strolled the square and sat with their people and watched the old women move in and out of the simple church with bunches of calla lilies picked fresh from beside the stream.

Then reaching far to one end, he sketched in Todos Santos, but not in the same detail. He had been there many times, but its memory was that of a man's and not as vivid as that of a boy.

The woods between the two places he knew well, and he traced the outline of an arroyo that filled only in the fall and a grove of giant walnut trees that he had watched carefully, harvesting the hard, oily nuts each winter. Once he found a giant limb splintered off from the rest of the tree by a windstorm and over a number of days carved a walnut bench for Tomasito (this before Efrán was even conceived), all of one piece. It had only added more fuel for the fire.

He warmed the last of his tortillas over the coals and surveyed his work. It was accurate, almost to scale, and he was pleased. It raised his mood to have a plan, one that he knew he could follow to its end.

He longed for a cup of hot coffee like Bonnie had each morning, and sometimes brought to him, thick and sweet and rich with cream. But he kicked out the fire and taking only his machete and his determination with him started toward Todos Santos, entering the woods exactly where he last had seen Leticia.

The woods had a way of reclaiming itself, healing the scars of feet and machetes in the same indifferent way, and Hector could see no sign of the panicky scramble and chase that had burst through the quietness just a few months before. Once again he relived the day, trying to gauge how far Leticia would have gone before the soldiers overtook her. He watched for a place where the ground had been scratched and gouged, tracks or remains or memories of bruises that the soft earth or the trees or the dry, misplaced leaves of the ground might remember.

But he found nothing.

He drank from the stream when he was thirsty and found nuts, scattered and neglected, under the high spread of trees.

Once he heard a shout and then another in the distance. They echoed through the woods, and he turned trying to locate their source, but then all was quiet except for the fussing of mountain jays.

That night, back at the ruins of his house, he lay exhausted under the moonless sky. He had filled himself with water from the spring and for the moment had forgotten his hunger, but he knew the next day he could not go on without food.

Suddenly Hector sensed something behind him. There had been no distinct noise, not the snap of a dry leaf or even the whistle of a tense breath, but he knew something had joined him. His hand eased its way slowly toward his machete.

Then a voice pushed through the night and Hector leaped to his feet. With a snap of his wrist he whipped the sheath of the machete from its blade.

"Hector," the voice from the darkness cracked with uncertainty. "Is that you?"

The voice moved toward him and became a man and then no more than a gangling boy. Hector waited silently.

"It is Paco," the voice said, and now Hector could see his face. "The son of Gabriel, your cousin."

Hector would no longer have known him, even in the light of morning, but he dropped his machete and embraced him until the boy awkwardly pushed away.

Then they sat and talked. Hector had neither drink nor food to offer, but he rebuilt the small fire so that they might see. From a small bundle Paco pulled a stringy chunk of dried goat meat that they shared while they talked. Paco told him how he had hidden when the soldiers came and why he stayed behind when his family hurried across the border.

"There is this girl," he said, and at that Hector hid a smile and nodded. "She lives in Chajul with her mother and I could not leave her, for we are to be married sometime soon, when there is sense and calm in the country again, when I can take the piece of land that has been promised me and begin to work it." He said these things for he had become a man. Hector saw that it was so.

Hector explained to Paco why he had come back and showed him the map that flickered with shadows on the smooth sand. With one hand he wiped across one-third of the woods. "There was no sign here, nothing, but tomorrow I will cover this," and he circled another third of the map with a stick.

Hector liked the way he had drawn the map. It gave him a plan and reassured him that he could rediscover a deliberate way to live his life. The same way he felt when he gazed out over a field of young corn, one that had become thick with weeds that the spring rains bring. When he began to hoe he only worked the row in front of him, not daring to look again at the whole field, knowing that the size of the task would overwhelm him. But at the end of the day he would stop and survey the rows and always felt surprise at the distance he had covered.

Paco studied the lines and curves in the sand and nodded. When he saw that the plan was good, he straightened up and spoke softly, carefully like a thoughtful man. He said that he would go with Hector, that the two of them could cover the ground more quickly, more thoroughly. He said that Leticia's disappearance was truly a mystery, for no one had seen her.

And that was not all. Three boys, all about Paco's

own age, were missing, too. It had taken a few weeks to discover that they had neither gone to Mexico with their families nor been taken in by friends or relatives. Some said that they had joined with the rebels and others said that, no, the brownshirts had forced them into the government army. No one knew the truth. Perhaps they had even been killed for revenge.

At that Hector shivered, feeling the blood that he had drawn from the soldiers flowing all through the country, sliding in a slow stream from the end of his machete as if it would never end.

"You should go to your father," Hector said. "He could use your energy and youth in San Caralampio, for his life is not easy. And there is danger for you here, especially if you are with me."

"Do not misunderstand me," Paco said with either embarrassment or amusement, which, in the dark Hector could not tell. "I will help you, for your search is honorable and right, but I am not staying here for you, and I will not leave for the sake of my father."

Hector nodded. He understood, for it seemed like no more than a long day since he had felt the same for Leticia.

They grew silent then for a long time, both moving to wherever they could find comfort in their minds.

Hector spent the night in a half-sleep, groping and searching through an impenetrable thicket. When he awoke the ground around him was scarred with his thrashing, as if he had slept with a herd of restless javalinas.

With Paco nearby the search for Leticia began to change. From both the small houses that clung tenaciously to the mountainsides and those that blended into the dense jungle of woods, people began to appear. At first they would acknowledge only Paco, although they all knew Hector and understood immediately why he had returned. They saw Paco as young and safe, not having offended the military. Still they talked guardedly and would hardly glance Hector's way. But later, as more and more of them appeared as if from nowhere, they began to include Hector, at first with a nod and then a polite shake of the hand, and by the third day, when word had flowed and spun its way all through the valley and across the mountains, with joyous hugs and promises of help. One boy had found a torn piece of a blouse, the embroidery tattered and faded. Could this be Leticia's, he asked. Hector took the scrap in his hands and turned it over and over, rubbing the texture with his fingers. But he could remember from the day she disappeared only the hurt and fear that patterned Leticia's face, and he was ashamed. You no longer even know what clothes your wife wore, he chastised himself. You no longer deserve a good and faithful wife. And he dreaded what his people must think of him now.

But he was wrong. From across the narrow valley old friends and cousins and nephews appeared, all eager to help, to do something, even if there was danger, for they had withdrawn into their own secret lives for so long that they had begun to feel like beaten, cowering dogs. Hector Rabinal is back! Hector Rabinal is back! We must help him find Leticia. The word spread like water on a flat rock and Hector could feel the spirits of the people explode like ground birds flushed from the edge of a wood.

With their husbands and sons the women sent Hector bags of food and blends of teas from roots and barks of trees. Hector found *milagros* and secret packets of herbs hidden among the tortillas and dried goat's meat. But nothing helped. There still was no sign of Leticia.

By the sixth night the map on the sand had been completely erased. Every gully and ravine between Huitupan and Todos Santos had been stirred and probed. As they sat around the fire Hector barely heard Paco's words as he talked. He told of a cousin he had seen that day who had by some good luck obtained a pair of Nike shoes and wore blue jeans with them just like they do in the north. Paco's voice was wistful yet full of hope as he described what he would soon provide for his bride-to-be in Chajul. But Hector saw the stories as foolish echoes of his own false hopes and hardly listened.

Then suddenly, as if he had been burned by a coal from the small fire, Hector leaped to his feet. He hurried to the ruin of his house and moved slowly around it. Paco watched in silence.

When Hector spoke it seemed to Paco as if the older man had been taken over by a strange spirit that could do no more than mumble to itself. "I know what I must do . . . yes . . . so simple . . . then she will know it is safe

. . . stronger, with braces from the heart of the trees." As he talked, Hector paced the ground by his house, over and over again calculating its length and the width with measured steps.

Finally Paco could stand it no longer, and he also jumped to his feet, demanding that Hector stop his mad pacing and explain what was happening.

"We will rebuild the house, just as it was before the fire. In that corner will be the place to cook and I will find a *comal* to replace the old one. The women will bring clothes, new ones that they have made, and lay them out by the mats that I will make. Leticia, wherever she is, no matter how far away, will hear of this and come out of hiding. Then she will know that it is no trick of the military to recapture her, that Hector Rabinal in truth has come back to protect her."

Paco started to protest, to tell Hector that Leticia was nowhere nearby or they would have known by now, that she was either dead (which he could never bring himself to say) or that she had been taken to a prison in some far-off city.

But Hector, with a wave of his hand and a glare silenced him.

"It is the only way. And I will find a team of oxen and begin to work my field, for it is time for corn and beans and squash to be sown together in the ground." Hector's steps grew longer and faster all at once and his voice took on the high pitch of a man who has been possessed, and Paco stepped back from the fire and watched from the shadow of the cliff.

Then Hector began to pull half-burned poles and clods of baked clay from the ruin of the house and pile them to one side. "Tomorrow," he said to Paco, "we will need shovels and carts to carry this all away," and he swept his arm about, as if with that gesture he could remove the entire past. "I will begin early. You will find help for me. When Leticia hears that her home has been restored she will come back. I know that she will." And with that Hector attacked the blackened remains like a man who had escaped from the house of smiles.

Paco did spread the word, and to his surprise, the people reacted with hope and belief. Yes, they said, that is a good plan. And the women set about weaving their favorite designs for Leticia to wear on her return. At noon the next day one man drove a team of oxen to Hector's field, and the men that showed up to rebuild the house numbered so many that they could hardly work for bumping into each other. Soon the earth was scraped clean and except for a little blackened clay the site was as when Hector first cleared it.

Hector moved constantly, shouting directions, digging into his memory for just the way things had been. Soon holes for the corner timbers were dug and from the upper reaches of the mountain burros dragged newly felled trees down the winding trails. The air was filled with the sounds of work, the men's voices carried a spirit they had not had for months. It was said that at night their wives lay beside them eagerly, as if their husbands had been transformed into the men they had first married.

Within only a few days Hector climbed to the peak of the house and secured the last sheath of straw for the roof. Below him, inside the house, he could hear the soft murmur of the women as they arranged and rearranged what Leticia would need when she returned.

From there Hector could see most of the valley and hear familiar sounds that had returned — the echo of an axe from the hillside above as someone gathered the week's firewood, children playing as their mothers knelt beside the stream and slapped wet clothes on the flat rocks. Even the dogs had become more playful, yelping and running with the young boys, no longer skittish and afraid.

Already he could see that the rows of his field had hints of yellow sprouts that had begun to push up through the rich soil.

Hector stood at the peak of the roof and stretched his full length, his arms extended. Then he turned silently, waving his arms in a slow crisscross pattern, a signal to all that he had returned, that the house and the field were his again, that Leticia could now return.

For several days more the women brought food and the men sat in the shade of the cliff with Hector or walked the young field with him, stooping to pull any weed that dared to invade. Paco proudly stayed near and explained to anyone who wandered by what Hector and his neighbors had done. At night the men brought *posh* and even some beer to celebrate their accomplishment. They told the stories of their fathers and grandfathers, stories that were familiar but had been buried for too long. They all knew, although no one would say it, that the story of Hector returning and resurrecting his house for his lost wife would enter into the stories of their sons and grandsons. Then one by one or in pairs they would leave, finding the trails that glowed in the moonlit nights and led them home.

Then only Paco would stay with Hector, both stretching out on woven mats under the stars, for Hector was saving the house for Leticia to see, not wanting even so much as a stray footprint to mark the hard-packed floor. With so much accomplished Hector found that words now flowed easily from him and he became as a boy again, relating to Paco all that had happened, all that he had seen in his journey to the north. And, also, Hector found himself inventing the future once again, how things would be with Leticia back once more.

One time Paco found the courage to ask what had to be hidden in the hearts of all the men. "And you are not afraid? Of the soldiers? That they will find that you are here?" Hector could only look at Paco in a puzzled sort of way, to hide the fear that always was there, and could not answer.

But after a week Leticia had not appeared and soon the women rarely showed up with food, having of necessity to fill their days once again with the needs of their own families. And the nights became quieter, more lonely, as the men and their drinks that gave comfort to the soul and a lift to the heart came less frequently. Then the visits stopped and still Hector and Paco waited.

Paco left twice a day to bring food and fetch water and firewood, but Hector could only wait and watch and listen. The yellow sprouts of corn in the field took on the green tops of mature plants and the stems of beans began to curve around them and the squash put out their runners and blanketed the ground. Still Hector waited. Still Leticia did not come.

Finally even the loyal Paco went into Chajul for two days to visit his *novia*. When he came back he brought rumors that soldiers were still in the area and had burned another village that was suspected of sympathizing with the rebels. Everywhere he went, Paco had been stopped. What is this we hear, he was asked. A miracle has occurred at Huitupan? A woman has returned from the dead? Paco tried to explain, but, as always, the people did not want to hear the truth but wanted more to believe in a miracle.

His *novia* finally became angry when they could no longer walk the quiet plaza of Chajul on a Sunday night and be left alone with their secret embraces. As it was, Paco had become a local celebrity because of his closeness to Hector and what had become known as the "miracle of Huitupan."

As Paco made his way back up the hill to Hector's he wondered how long this could go on. His *novia* had denied him the favor of stroking her breasts before he left and made no promises for the future. How she could play games with him, when he was finally involved in something so serious as the possible reappearance of Leticia, he could not know. A man's work must come first and for now Paco's work was to help Hector, to stand beside him, wait with him until there was no longer any hope. But to abandon him for the silly whim of a *novia* would never do. He would discuss this with Hector that very night, for it was not the sort of thing a friend would hear or understand, not without making a big joke of it. Besides, Hector knew more about women than any man in the village; he could tell from the way the story of Bonnie was unfolding that there would be more to it than just the strangeness of having a woman as a *patrón*.

As Paco neared the flat of the hill that held Hector's house he stopped and listened. He could hear the faint grind of a truck near the village, an unfamiliar sound, not that of either of the only two trucks that he knew so well. One came always on Friday and struggled up the rugged, narrow trail carrying cases of *cerveza*. The other had been there last week with a month's supply of Pepsi and wouldn't be back for a few weeks. This was different. But the sound died away and so Paco turned to climb the last few gravelly steps to the top once more. Then he froze.

From above Paco could hear voices, incoherent at first, but then very clearly Hector's voice rang out through the late afternoon. "Where is my wife? What have you done to her? Take me to her, you sons of cowardly dogs!" Then a voice saying "Quiet, you traitor! You will join your wife soon enough." And then a thud and then another and a moan. Then Paco heard a laugh and several voices squabbling as if arguing what to do.

Paco fought off the initial panic that flowed through him. Then he moved a few steps off the path and knelt quietly and waited. When the voices didn't stop, he crept on his belly slowly upward until he could see first the roof of Hector's new house and then the yard and the half dozen men that seemed to fill it.

Brownshirts! Paco could plainly see the outline of a white hand on their backs. Hector was on the ground, his hands tied behind his back. He was no longer making a sound, but Paco could see him rock slowly from side to side as if in pain.

Paco's first impulse was to go for help, but there were only his uncles and cousins and no one had so much as a revolver, and the soldiers all carried rifles. Paco had never felt the aloneness he then felt, the helplessness of being a man and knowing what should be done, what was the right thing to do, but being absolutely impotent to act. He could charge forward and be killed or captured; he could run for help, but there was none, or he could warn the village to hide. But then he remembered the truck he had heard and figured that the village was already warned — perhaps too late.

And even then, as he looked back through the valley he could see more fires than usual, some with angry black smoke, and he knew that to go there would be futile. So Paco did the only thing he could. He watched and waited, hoping as if in a dream for a miracle to happen.

Finally the soldiers reached some kind of agreement and lifted Hector across the back of a burro and began to lead him down the trail toward Huitupan. They passed within a few feet of Paco. For a few minutes he remained flat on his belly, not daring to move. Then, no longer content to be a lowly cowardly snake, he found the familiar trail and followed as a lonely witness to the plodding procession as it made its way toward Huitupan.

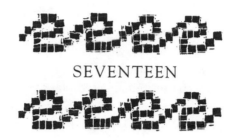

SEVENTEEN

HECTOR welcomed the time that Paco spent in Huitupan with his *novia*, partly because it helped him relive some of the same days he had spent courting Leticia. That had been only a few years back, perhaps more than it seemed to him, but everything was changing. The young men now carried radios while they strolled with their *novias*, and music of the north boomed from them while they walked the *parque*. No longer was it necessary for an older sister or an aunt to be with them, turning her head away at the right moments to allow just long enough for quick embraces and furtive kisses.

No, it was different now. But then, nothing had

stayed the same. Hector used his time alone to stare out over the valley and search his soul for the right answer to the only important question that he knew, one that he and Father Cota had wrestled with for hours when Hector was still young and felt himself overflowing with answers. The question had seemed silly to him then, one of Father Cota's word games set up to trick him. But now Hector saw it differently. Father Cota had posed it this way: "Hector," he would say when they were quiet and alone, "what does it mean to be a man?" The question seemed so simple then that it had angered Hector, but the more he struggled with the answer, the larger the question grew, Father Cota enlarging it and herding Hector's confident answers toward foolish conclusions.

Now Hector could see where Father Cota had been leading him — to a place where only he, Hector Rabinal, could answer, not with words, but with action, or, even as now, with inaction. With waiting.

After awhile Hector became restless with the quiet and tired from his mind carrying him in so many circles. He wished Paco would return with food and news from Chajul. If he only knew more, then, perhaps, he could make the right choices. Not only for himself, but for his boys back in San Caralampio.

Then he turned toward his newly rebuilt house. I will build a fire, he thought, inside the house, just the way Leticia would have. This was some vague impulse — perhaps he thought that a fire would make the house more visible or perhaps he only wanted to test the roof, to see that smoke would draw from one end and not find its way through the open door.

As he gathered kindling outside he heard something above, on the side of the hill, and thought that Paco might have cut across the mountain straight from Chajul, which was a quicker way to come back, a way that saved going through Huitupan, although it was rugged and not for old men.

Hector's arms were full of split limbs for the fire and he had just straightened up when the blow came, catching him at the base of his skull and from then on his world spun in a descending whirl, one where voices, even his own, confused him. As he fell he did see the brownshirts even before he fully felt the butt of the gun at his head. He remembered even in his own pain crying out at them, raising himself half way from the ground, demanding, as if he had any right to demand, that they lead him to Leticia. His words echoed against the rock cliff and mixed with their shouts and then he heard as much as felt another thud, and Hector tasted blood blended with the blackened sand where he lay.

Their words flowed around him then and he found that he had given himself over to them, or perhaps to something else that he could not define. It did not matter. His life was no longer his and he was filled with a mixture of fear and a strange sense of relief.

Then he was across the back of a burro, his hands and feet tied together with a rope that looped under the burro's belly. Hector found himself no longer in pain, but terribly conscious of each step the burro took, of each turn in the trail, as the caravan descended slowly into Huitupan.

At a curve in the trail one of the soldiers jerked the burro to a stop and turned it sideways. Then he pulled Hector's head around so that he could see the house above him, and once again Hector could only watch the flames as they seared through the roof.

Finally they reached level ground, and the burro's hooves clattered on the stones that paved the square around the *parque*. The soldiers fired their rifles into the air and for the first time in months the church bells began to ring. The six soldiers then were joined by others, those who had been in the truck that Paco heard. They marched together around the small plaza and as they marched and fired their guns they shouted, "Hector Rabinal is back, Hector Rabinal is back. Come and see. Hector Rabinal is back."

Then they laughed and took Hector down. They tied the rope from his feet to the wooden saddle of the burro and led the animal slowly around the *parque*, dragging Hector around the rough street over and over again. All the while the soldiers went from house to house, forcing the women and their children to watch the procession. The men stopped their work in the fields and joined them, the machetes at their side as useless as toys.

Later the soldiers ran from house to house, and store to store, tossing torches onto the roofs. The women fought and the children screamed. One man tried to save his store — it had been his grandfather's — by jerking the torch from a soldier's grip and he was shot down like a worthless animal.

Then the brownshirts led the burro, still dragging its bloody load, to the gazebo in the center of the *parque*. There they tossed the rope across the gazebo's open beams and hoisted Hector Rabinal up by his ankles, and there he spun slowly, winding the rope first one way and then slowly unwinding the other. Hector could see Huitupan as it burned, then he felt something at his throat. There was no longer pain — he was beyond the point of pain — and blood flowed across one eye.

A yellow dog, all ribs and teats that flapped across the stone floor of the gazebo, wandered around Hector as he slowly turned. The last thing he saw, before his other eye was covered with blood from the slash at his throat was the yellow dog hungrily lapping up his blood where it pooled on the gazebo floor.

Those who were witnesses later swore that at that moment a smile crossed Hector's face and remained there even after his world had turned to blackness. It was a smile, some said, as if Hector had asked a question, and then had been surprised by the simple answer.